An Anthology of Christmas Murders

Terror, Tinsel and Turkey

Edited by Jeremy Moiser

PNEUMA SPRINGS PUBLISHING UK

First Published in 2014 by:
Pneuma Springs Publishing

An Anthology of Christmas Murders - Terror, Tinsel and Turkey
Copyright © 2014 Annie Coyle Martin, Julius Falconer, Peter Good,
Peter Hodgson, Neal James, James McCarthy, Andrew Malloy, Steve
Morris, Harry Riley, Derek Rosser
ISBN13: 9781782283577

British Library Cataloguing in Publication Data. A catalogue record for
this book is available from the British Library.

Pneuma Springs Publishing
A Subsidiary of Pneuma Springs Ltd.
7 Groveherst Road, Dartford Kent, DA1 5JD.
E: admin@pneumasprings.co.uk
W: www.pneumasprings.co.uk

This is a work of fiction. Names, characters, places and incidents are either
products of the author's imagination or are used fictitiously. Any resemblance to
actual events or locales or persons, living or dead, save those clearly in the public
domain, is purely coincidental.

To all Pneuma Springs authors

ACKNOWLEDGEMENT

Thanks to all the anthology contributors for being a joy to work with.

Alone we can do so little;
Together we can do so much
- Helen Keller

CONTENTS

Christmas at the Smooth Rock Motel
Annie Coyle Martin

May I tell you a story? A Christmas story? I can't vouch for its, shall we say, historical accuracy in every detail, although I can assure you that I was sufficiently close to the events to be able to vouch for at least some of them. The rest I've reconstructed as an imaginative surplus! It doesn't really matter at this point who I am. Think of me as Tom, if it helps: Tom, Dick or Harry. The events I'm going to tell you about took place in Quebec province – where it always snows plentifully at Christmas and Santa Claus has a hard job getting about – a few years ago. It's not a particularly uplifting story; but then most of life isn't uplifting, is it? It's time the record was set straight. So, are you sitting comfortably? Then I shall begin.

Linda McCallum, one of the two housekeeping staff in charge of guest bedrooms at the Smooth Rock Motel, not all that far from where I'm sitting now, made her way along the second floor pushing her cart with its container for used sheets and other bed linen and its shelves of fresh supplies. She checked her list. All ten rooms on the second floor were to be occupied. It was December 23rd, and the motel was quiet. It was eleven o'clock now, and most of the guests would have checked out. But for that evening many more rooms were booked - she didn't know how many – but she expected quite a few: skiers arriving for a Christmas break. The bar off the lobby would be busy early in the evening, but skiers retired relatively early after dinner and a modest amount of alcohol.

The Smooth Rock Motel could not rival its bigger and more expensive brothers, better placed in the resort, but it boasted a steady all-year-round trade. At Christmas especially, it could almost be guaranteed to be full. And it occasionally had its small share of drama, as you shall hear.

At Christmas, guests were liberal with their tips, and when Linda came to check the rooms after the holiday, December 27th, she would find on the bedside table a generous tip left by the departing guests. Nearly all the rooms would be taken. Linda liked to be busy - and to construct stories in her mind about the guests - stories about couples who booked separate rooms; guests with the same name in different rooms; people seemingly totally on their own; and those who booked the same room despite different names: lovers stealing a weekend away, or so she thought. And the guests who left the rooms in a mess - empty beer bottles, waste baskets overflowing with Scotties tissues, empty cigarette packets ...

She checked the empty rooms first, just opening each door and glancing inside. At room 215, she walked in, went over to the window and looked out on the snowy landscape now bathed in bright sunlight. This morning, when she awoke in the room she shared with Marie, it had been dark, gloomy. Now it seemed spring was on its way. It was so beautiful it brought back memories of her country childhood, building snow-forts and snowmen with her brothers in the Quebec countryside. In January, when things quieted down, she would have days off to make up for the extra hours she worked over Christmas. Then she and Marie would go cross-country skiing or snow-shoeing. Linda could hardly wait. They would have liked to try downhill, but the fees were too high. And Linda didn't see the point of racing down the same hills time after time. Better to spend the day seeing the countryside.

She now started on the rooms that had been occupied. She checked room 216 first. There was no tag on the door handle to indicate whether the room was to be cleaned. She knocked twice - no answer. She used her card to enter. Someone was lying in the bed, slightly turned away from the door.

'Excuse me. I thought you'd checked out.' No answer. 'Are you all right?'

She approached closer and saw the woman lying motionless, shocking in death, her eyes open, her tongue slack, protruding, saliva dry over her chin, her face purple.

'Oh, lor'!' Linda stood riveted for a few seconds, then turned and ran sobbing out of the door. She ran along the corridor past the elevator. She slammed the stairs door open and, hanging desperately on to the railing, stumbled down the stairs and across the lobby. She burst into the office of Anna Hayman, the hotel manager. 'Miss Hayman, there's a woman dead in 216.' Miss Hayman was fleshy and faded but had clearly once been an attractive woman.

'What?' she said.

'Miss Hayman, Miss Hayman, I found a woman dead in 216.' Linda clung to the door of Miss Hayman's office, pale, breathless.

'Good heavens! Are you sure she's dead?'

'I'm sure, I'm sure.'

'Sit down.' She directed Linda to a chair in the corner of her office. Linda sat with her face in her hands. Her dark good looks suggested, despite her name, a Spanish, or at least southern Mediterranean, background. Canada has long been proud to host people from all over the world who wish to share her values and life-style. (I speak as a Canadian, of course!) 'Have you got your door-card, Linda?' Linda gave it over, her hand shaking. She could not remember shutting the door. Miss Hayman went to the door of her office. 'Larry, I want you here,' she called. The tall fair-haired young man who manned the reception desk came over, and Miss Hayman handed him the card. 'Check Room 216: Linda here says the woman there's dead – if you don't mind, that is.' He took the card and walked to the elevator. 'Linda,' she went on, turning to the chambermaid, 'you've had a shock. Sit there, and I'll make you a coffee. Do you take sugar?' Linda nodded, her face pale, miserable. She sat there, seeing in her mind the woman strangled with the scarf, saliva dried on her chin, her eyes open, rolled up in her head. She saw that Miss Hayman looked almost as if she herself had found the body - shocked but, as manageress, trying to keep going and in her mind running through the actions she ought to be taking. The manageress plugged in the coffee machine in her office.

When Larry checked room 216, the door was open. He entered, glanced at the corpse, left and checked that the door had locked.

He took the elevator downstairs, crossed the lobby and nodded at Miss Hayman. The latter asked:

'Is she really dead?'

'Seems so'

'Go back to your desk.'

'Right, Miss Hayman' Miss Hayman thought he seemed very cool for a man who had just seen a murdered woman. Miss Hayman shut the door of her office and dialled 911 from the telephone on her desk. The dispatcher answered immediately.

'Ambulance or police?'

'Police, police!'

'Where are you?'

'At the Smooth Rock Motel on Mountain Road.'

'Stay on the line.' Anna Hayman hung on to the receiver. She would have to contact Frederick Johnson, the motel owner, who was off on some trapping expedition or other. Then she heard the sirens. 'You can hang up now,' the dispatcher was telling her. She hung up. The sirens were getting closer. In a matter of minutes, she saw the lights, and two police cars were coming across the parking lot, and then they parked at the entrance. Miss Hayman walked out and stood at reception. A detective corporal and two detective constables walked into the lobby. The corporal flashed his badge. He was, she thought, well, not to put too fine a point on it, too weedy to be a policeman. The constables, on the other hand, were both tall and well-built, with chests and shoulders bursting out of their uniforms.

'Detective Corporal Crosby, ma'am. And you are - ?'

'Anna Hayman, the motel manager.'

'You called 911.'

'Yes, we've discovered a dead woman here. She was murdered.'

'Murdered? They didn't tell us that at the switchboard. How do you know?'

'Not difficult, officer,' she answered, summoning up a sort of wry smile. 'She apparently has a scarf tied tight round her neck.

Her eyes are open, but I'm told there's no doubt she's dead – none whatever.'

'I see. Who found her?'

'Linda McCallum, one of the housekeeping staff.'

'I see,' Crosby said again, noting the fact down. 'Miss Hayman, how many exits are there in this building beside the main one?'

'Two at the back, at each end of the building.'

'Do you have locks for those doors?'

'Yes, but they're never locked. In case of emergency, you know. They open from the inside.'

'We'd like those keys.' Anna went into her office and took the keys from her desk drawer. She handed them to the policeman. 'Are these the only keys?'

'No, the owner has a set to allow him to come and go to his apartment, which is on the first floor behind the elevator.'

'Thank you.' The corporal thought Miss Hayman looked exhausted. He felt a little sorry for her. What a shock for the poor woman! He gave the keys to one of the other officers, who made his way toward the back stairs to lock the doors. The other officer left, and Miss Hayman could see him begin to set up police tape round the front entrance. A short time later she saw a large black van with white lettering - 'Forensic Identification Unit' - park outside the door. 'Now, Miss Hayman,' Officer Crosby said, 'we need to see your list of guests. And we'll need a list of all your staff and to interview them. I'm locking all outside doors – just as a precaution, you understand. For the moment. There's no chance the murderer's stayed behind waiting for us to arrive! But you never know.'

'Most guests have checked out.'

'We don't necessarily have to see them all now, but we may contact them later. Who are the owners here? We'll need to see them.'

'The owner's away on a trip. I need to contact him to tell him this awful news.'

'Who is he?'

'Frederick Johnson. Lives in Quebec. Has business interests in the city as well as here – but he won't be back till after New Year.'

'Do you know how to get in touch with him? Where's he staying?'

'Don't know. Camping out somewhere, if what he told me was true; or perhaps a log-cabin. I have his cell-phone number. I am not looking forward to telling him. For the list of guests, it's best you go over the register. Larry at reception will do that with you, if that's OK.'

'Another officer will begin that.' Crosby walked to the door and called the policeman who had set up the police tape. 'This is Detective Constable Decker,' he told Larry. 'Andy, I need you to go over the register and develop a list with Larry here. We need the time when each guest arrived, what room they occupied etc. And of course any that have checked out already. We'll need to check them all, and of course the staff.'

'OK, we'll get on with that right away.'

'Good. Then send it over - email it - to the station, and we'll have it checked to see whether any have a record.' He returned to the manageress.

'What can you tell me of the victim's movements last night, Miss Hayman?'

'Nothing,' she said. 'She came for a three-day skiing trip, as I recall. What most people do is get back from the slopes, shower, have a drink at the bar, go along to dinner in the restaurant, then spend what's left of the evening watching TV, chatting, playing cards – but you know all this as well as I do, officer. I suppose the dead girl did the same last night – but I don't know.'

'Can anybody get into the motel from outside during the night?'

'Yes, if they want to,' Anna answered wearily. 'We have a night porter, but someone could get past him if they tried hard enough. We rely on guests to lock themselves securely into their rooms. The doors can't be opened from the corridor without a card.'

'So the victim let her aggressor into her room?'

'Looks like it, doesn't it, officer?' Anna managed, 'but that's not going to be very helpful, is it? Anybody could knock, claiming to be room service, say, and once the door's open, well … Our guests don't expect crime here: we're a law-abiding community.'

'The murderer may have made a noise in overpowering his victim. We'll have to check that. Nobody mentioned anything to you?'

'No.'

'Strangled with a scarf, you say? Not easy to strangle someone with a scarf: generally too soft. It'd need to be a thin material, the sort that twists into a kind of rope. Doesn't it make a man more likely? Strangling someone needs quite a bit of strength, you know.' However, he could see that this sort of detail was unsettling the manageress, even more than she was unsettled already.

Anna watched through her office door as total strangers took over the motel. She imagined the forensic team in their white cover-up suits and gloves working through the room where the woman had been found dead. She imagined a systematic sweep of the premises by uniformed policemen. She imagined stray guests being accosted and asked for a detailed account of their movements.

'Look, I'll have to call Mr Johnson,' she told Officer Crosby. 'He won't like it: a girl murdered in his motel! I dread the effect on him. He's known for his fits of rage if things don't go smoothly, and my job could be on the line - not that the murder's my fault, of course!' She hastened to add that she normally got on well with the owner. She was well paid and had a comfortable bed-sitting room at the back of the motel. She had a good job, and he treated her respectfully.

'Who's the dead girl, by the way?' Crosby asked.

'Louise Laval. I've checked the register. She was apparently from a town called Pointe Jacques, about fifty kilometres away. Nice bit of country, that: I happen to know it, because my great-grandpa was born there. Sorry: more important things to talk about, officer. Louise's poor family: they'll be shocked, won't they? Can I ask you to give them the bad news: I'm not sure I could face it.'

'Sure.'

'And we'll have to consider the effect of this tragedy on the staff – and I suppose on the business. Soon the press'll arrive, and that'll mean bad publicity. What holiday-goer's going to want to stay where there's been a murder? Look, I think I'll gather the staff in a meeting, to talk to them and tell them all's in good hands.' She ventured a weak smile in Crosby's direction. 'What do I tell the new guests? Although they won't probably be arriving till four, I'm worried.' Then she added: 'Sorry again, officer. Here I am, fretting about the business, and there's a woman dead, a young woman.'

'You were going to phone the owner, remember?'

'Oh, yes, I'll do that now. He'll be particularly shocked, as I think he knew the girl.'

'Oh?'

'That was the impression I got when I saw them together on the evening of her arrival. Perhaps it was me imagining things.' Frederick Johnson had gone away with a friend on some hunting trip in a remote part of Manitoba, she'd thought, as she tried to remember what he had told her. Porcupine Forest? Somewhere like that? She did not know anything more. 'Excuse me, officer.'

'Of course. I'll take the opportunity to go up to room 216, if I may.'

Anna went into her office. Linda was still sitting there, pale and nervous, waiting for the police to interview her. 'Linda, I must call the boss and tell him.' Linda got up to leave. 'Stay where you are,' she instructed gently. 'He might want to talk to you.' Linda sat down. Of course, although he would no doubt be distressed at the girl's untimely death, he might welcome the publicity it engendered, and Anna was not sure she could cope with that. She hesitated. Eventually she dialled his cell-number. She almost felt relief when there was no answer. She would call him again in an hour or so. She imagined him deep in some forest, stalking game in deadly silence. Of course, he would have turned off his phone. Or perhaps there was no signal. Anna was tense, she knew that, and that was not helpful in present circumstances: the occasion called not for feminine panic but for calm efficiency. 'Linda, watch things here. I'm going to check the coffee shop, to provide our, um, visitors with at least an appearance of normality. If you want a coffee, help yourself, of course. Might calm your nerves a bit.' Linda shook her head, and Anna Hayman, trying to appear in control, went to the small coffee shop, off the lobby.

The restaurant at the back of the coffee shop was closed. It would open in the evening when the motel got going properly. Or would it? Yes, it would! She had to ensure as much normality as possible, if the motel's reputation were not to suffer unduly. She only hoped the police would be as unobtrusive and as speedy as possible. Dared she hope that they might be out of the way by four o'clock? She must remember to ask Crosby. In the coffee shop, she bought a doughnut and a coffee. Finn, the coffee-shop attendant, handed her the doughnut and watched as she filled a paper cup with coffee from the machine. He whispered:

'Anna, what on earth's going on? What are the police doing here?'

'We found a dead woman upstairs.'

'Crikey! You don't say! That's awful. Who is it?'

'A young woman; a guest in room 216. Here on her own for a few days' skiing.'

'An accident?'

'No. I'm afraid it's murder.'

'Murder?' He paused as the word sank in, his face registering his sense of shock. 'That's terrible! Anything I can do? Look, Anna, I'll close the shop up.' His face was pale, frightened.

'No, you're to stay open – as normal as possible. Things must go on. In any case, the police and the forensic team may well want coffee.'

'OK. S'pose so.' But it was obvious, as his expression altered, that he felt he was missing out. Did you ever read *Bugsy Malone*? Chapter I ends with the words, 'Whatever game it was that everyone was playing, sure as eggs is eggs, Roxy Robinson was out of it'. That's evidently how Finn felt! He sighed and began to wipe the counter furiously.

'Finn, the cops will want to talk to you, too.' A small consolation, he supposed. He scrubbed the counter harder.

She knew she had to try to reach Frederick. She dialled his cellphone again. No answer. Of course, it was probably only a little over an hour since she had tried before. She left a message for him to call her. She saw that the forensic unit were leaving now, the body in a bag on the stretcher, the towels and sheets from the victim's room in a clear plastic bag. Well, thank heaven for that! The motel seemed to be quieting down a little, even sooner than she had hoped.

Two hours later, Detective sergeant Mike Savage arrived to oversee operations. He asked for a room he could use as a base, and Anna found a parlour at the back of the motel which would not interfere with motel business. Crosby briefed the sergeant and then said:

'Forensic have already submitted a preliminary report.' He handed Savage a sheet of paper. 'They're still working on things, of course, but there's apparently no doubt about the cause of death – strangulation by means of a ligature - and the victim was pregnant. From what we've learned so far,' he went on, 'except for Larry Jones, the night receptionist and porter, none of the people who stayed here or on the staff has ever been convicted of a criminal offence. Nor was Larry Jones convicted, although he was charged four years ago with assaulting a young woman in Montreal. However, the young woman withdrew her complaint. Case kept on file. There must have been considerable evidence against him for the police to retain the record of his arrest, but, of course, a man's innocent until proved guilty, isn't that so, sarge? Now, one other thing to fill you in on. The manageress – Anna Somebody-or-Other - suspects that the dead girl and the owner of the motel were acquainted: saw them together on the evening of her arrival. We haven't checked the owner's apartment, and there's probably no need, but I suppose we'll be accused of dereliction of duty, irresponsibility, cutting corners, lack of foresight, failure to observe routine – '

'Yes, yes, I get your drift. So we'll ask for a warrant to search his apartment, and then a locksmith can come and open the door for us – save us smashing it in, I suppose. Always upsets people, that – I can hardly blame 'em. Untidy, as well. While we're about it, if the manageress hasn't caught up with Johnson, perhaps we should have a go. Find out exactly where he's holidaying and get hold of him. It's best he gets back here, anyway. It'll take a few days, maybe a week, to get the warrant, especially at Christmas, so it'll save a lot of time if we get him back to the motel. I want to let the place get back to normal as soon as possible: mustn't be thought to be damaging a local business, you know!' And with that he left.

Fifty kilometres west of the Smooth Rock Motel, Julie Laval, the dead woman's fifty-five-year-old mother, was well into her day as the cook at 'The Sunrise', the only restaurant in the little town of Pointe Jacques, although on the highway leading to the village there were several roadside eating places: Harvey's, Subway, MacDonald's and another which did a brisk take-away service. The Sunrise was a thriving business, and Julie appreciated that, as well as the fact that it was only a short walk from her home. She shared the house with her daughter Louise, who had a one-bedroom apartment on the second floor with a separate entrance at the side of the house. Louise had lived in Montreal for a short time several years earlier but came home when her application to work in the bank in Pointe Jacques was accepted: steady, well-rewarded employment, and Julie was proud of her only child. Although a widow, Julie was never lonely. Her brother and his family lived nearby, and she kept up with her friends, volunteered at the local food-bank and belonged to a book club and a bridge club. She prided herself on allowing Louise complete independence: after all, she was twenty-seven years old. Louise paid the rent on time; they had an affectionate relationship, and Julie often said how lucky she was to have her as her daughter. Louise entertained friends in her apartment, and Julie could sometimes hear the sound of a movie they were watching or a program on television. There was sometimes a black Cadillac parked outside. Julie believed in not asking question about who it was her daughter entertained. Sometimes she saw a delivery person bringing food from the take-out restaurant on the highway. They were never noisy or loud late at night. In fact, it was a perfect arrangement. The Sunrise would close early tomorrow, after lunch, giving the staff Christmas Day and December 26th off. Julie had a robust Christmas dinner planned for herself and Louise. Louise was taking a few days off, and yesterday she had left with her skis and her ski clothes for an outing. She would be back tomorrow.

It was now four thirty, and Jody Harper, the chief of forensics, and his staff had finished the first stage of work on Louise Laval's remains. She seemed a healthy woman, and there was no sign of injury that would have preceded her murder. She was pregnant, he estimated three months. He had agreed to telephone Detective sergeant Savage when he had finished the next stage of his investigation – although he did not expect to be in for any surprise - but felt that they would have to delay much of the work till after the holiday.

Detective sergeant Savage indicated to most of his officers that they could leave their posts, as he believed nothing more could be done till after Christmas. Most of the necessary forensic work had been completed. He assured Miss Hayman that another officer would take over and stay – just in case! - but he felt things should be discrete and that the motel should be allowed to carry on as normal. Anna Hayman having approached Detective Constable Crosby and explained that guests booked for Christmas were beginning to arrive, Crosby conveyed her concerns to his boss. Anna was very tired: she always counted on having a break in the afternoon, and she had not been able to take one. She was on tenterhooks. She had allowed the housekeeping staff to leave as usual.

The young woman who would work evening shift as deputy manager and general point-of-call arrived at five, and Anna told her of the events that had occurred.

'Of course, Tess, the police are on top of things, and we're getting back to normal.'

'Good heavens! Will I be on my own, Miss Hayman?'

'Not at all! Pat will be here as usual.' Pat was the night porter. 'As well, the sergeant in charge of the case told me I can open the bar as usual at six and the restaurant. The staff will be here soon. And there's to be a constable on the premises overnight, so you'll be fine.' Although Anna spoke with confidence, she did not feel confident.

Two junior policemen, Pat Quan and Ben Shields, who had been sent to inform Judy Laval that her daughter had been murdered, arrived at Pointe Jacques. There was no answer at Louise Laval' address given in the register at the hotel. Pat Quan, the younger of the two officers, knocked on the door of the house next door. The woman who answered directed them to The Sunrise Restaurant:

'That's where her mother works: she's the cook there. You must have passed it on the way in.' They thanked her, and, as they set out for the restaurant, Pat told his colleague:

'I hate this, Ben.'

'Me too. Let's talk to the manager first.' When they arrived at The Sunrise Restaurant, the manager invited them into his office, and, when they told him that Judy Laval's daughter had been murdered, he called Judy in and, as gently as they could, the policemen told her that her daughter had murdered. She was deeply shocked, speechless. Then she said through her tears:

'I shouldn't have let her go. That Johnson - I never trusted him. I tried to persuade my poor girl to go skiing somewhere else, but she told me she liked the Smooth Rock and that in any case the owner would be away on a trip of his own. None of this would've happened if I'd let her stay in Montreal, but I wanted her near home.' She sobbed uncontrollably. After a pause, she went on:

'She loved Montreal, you know, but I was getting old and lonely and wanted to see her more often, to have her by me.'

'And how long's she been here now?'

'Four years – and I thought all was going so well!' She sobbed. The police wanted to ask her some questions, but this was not the time. The restaurant manager telephoned his wife and asked her to come and stay with Judy. The police left, their unsavoury task completed with as much gentleness and tact as they had been able to muster. Informing someone of the sudden and violent death of a close relative must be one of the worst duties an officer was ever called on to fulfil; of a daughter, even worse. Dealing with bank robbers, muggers, thieves and rapists was easy in comparison.

'Thank God that's done,' Patrick Quan said as they left.

'Poor woman!' Ben Shields replied. They sat in the car, compared notes and prepared a report for Detective sergeant Savage. Now the police work, to the extent possible, was deferred till December 27th. The room where the victim had been found, now empty with the desolation of violent death, was locked and sealed, and the police retained the admission card.

Turning the keys over to Janice Murray, who arrived at five thirty, Miss Hayman explained the happenings of the day. Janice would be in charge till just after midnight. Miss Hayman was not surprised that she knew about the tragedy. The CBC had covered the story at five o'clock and referred to it as 'breaking news' but had no details, since the reporter who had gone to the motel was met by the police at the entrance and had been told the investigation was under way. No other details had been provided. The motel continued with business as usual, and Anna was confident that the new guests would notice nothing untoward.

And so Christmas passed: breakfasts in the diner overlooking the valley, skiing all day on the slopes, thrills and spills, flirting, new friendships, a festive dinner in the evening and loud bustling après-ski conviviality before an early night.

On December 27th, the police resumed a fully-fledged investigation. Linda started her vacation but was told she had to keep the police informed of her whereabouts, as had Larry Jones. Although Larry Jones had not been convicted of a crime in Montreal, merely arrested, the police, considering his presence in Montreal and Constable Quan's report, which noted that the victim had been in Montreal about the same time, interviewed Larry Jones, who denied knowing the victim or ever having met her. The police, however, insisted on getting a DNA sample. Larry

Jones provided one without protest. Savage quizzed him mercilessly on his movements on the night in question. Where was he, when, why, who could vouch for his movements? and so on. The victim had not been sexually assaulted, there was none of Jones' DNA on the body, no shadow of a motive could be plausibly advanced. When checked against the strands of hair on the victim's hands, Jones' DNA came up negative. Savage had, after his long interview, suspected that it would, but he still considered Jones a suspect. Had to. Other evidence would be needed, which even a clever lawyer could not turn to his client's advantage. He ordered a full background report on the young man and left it at that for the moment.

By December 28th, Johnson had still not been located. To Anna, he was deliberately avoiding answering his phone: it was inconceivable that he had not once contacted her to ask whether all was well at the motel. She even felt moved to express her concerns to the detective. A warrant to search Frederick Johnson's apartment had been secured, and Detective sergeant Savage had called for a locksmith to open the door. The locksmith had also made two keys for the door and handed them to Savage. The latter felt that his suspicions were moving in one direction. He watched Jody Harper and one of his staff comb through Frederic's apartment. Jody was extremely proud of his proficiency in DNA, and there was plenty of scope to gather evidence: a toothbrush, an unwashed coffee cup, used tissues in a waste basket.

'I won't conceal from you, Miss Hayman, that it's looking more and more probable that your Mr Johnson had a hand in this. Only fair to warn you.'

'Mr Johnson? Oh, no, surely not!' she exclaimed. 'He wouldn't do anything like that. Just not his style. I won't believe it. He did play around a bit – if you get my meaning – but, no, not this.'

'Then how do you explain that it was his scarf round the girl's neck?'

'Was it? Anyone could have picked it up if he'd left it lying around.'

'Well, we're keeping an open mind, and the investigation's far from complete. But I just thought you should know.'

'Thank you, officer,' she said, with wonderment in her voice.

'I understand that border services have responded,' Harper commented to Savage a few minutes later, as he was leaving, 'and that this guy never crossed the border into the US. So where is he?'

'Heaven knows. Canada's a big place, you know, and, if he's gone hunting or trapping with his buddies, they could be deep in some very inhospitable places. We'll find him: we generally do. It's astonishing how many people think they can just disappear. Some do, of course, and only close family worry about them. But once the police put their minds to it, it's not easy to avoid detection. All faces are different, Jody, as you well know, and these days no one can hide for ever, whether he's in a crowd or out on his ownsome-lonesome.'

'Yeah, I'm sure you'll find him. Not really my business, anyway. Well, I'm going to do a reverse paternity test on his DNA and the victim's, to see whether he's father of the victim's unborn child.'

'New one on me. What is it?'

'I'll explain,' and Jody and traced a chart on a page of his notebook, three rows, one headed 'father', the next 'child', and the third 'mother' and explained the calculations that would yield the finding. 'It's a way of working out who a child's father is when the father isn't available for DNA testing.' Savage was intrigued. Finally they were finished. 'I'll be in touch, Mike.' And Jody and his assistant packed up their equipment.

On December 29th, they reported their findings to the sergeant. They had concluded that Frederick Johnson was not only the father of the victim's unborn child but had most likely killed her. The DNA evidence found in his apartment matched that found in hairs in the victim's hands. A more concentrated search for him would be started, and the reporter from the local paper, who had just arrived again, was informed by Savage that Frederick Johnson was the principal 'person of interest'. The news that Frederick Johnson was wanted by the police quickly spread. Every police station in Canada was on the lookout for him. His car licence number was on every police website. The police announced that he was their chief suspect, or, as expressed in police-speak, 'they were anxious to trace Mr Johnson as an important witness'.

Savage sat down to consider the case. The three requirements the jury would be looking for were motive, means and opportunity. Everyone, even schoolboys – and schoolgirls, too, he supposed - knew that! Well, Johnson had the means. It was one of his scarves that had been used to silence the victim. But was that not suspicious in itself? Why would Johnson leave so flagrant a clue behind? He also had the opportunity: he had been at the motel on the night of the 23rd-24th December, leaving for his vacation in the woods only on Christmas Eve. Motive? Well, he had got a girl pregnant. Perhaps this was inconvenient. Perhaps it would interfere with his relationship with any other bird he had in tow. Perhaps Louise had dumped him. Yes, there were possibilities, but somehow it did not seem to hang together. And the evidence against him was slender: a clever lawyer would make mincemeat of a few strands of his hair clutched in the victim's hand. All right, he was the father of Louise's baby – but that didn't make him a murderer.

Larry Jones, then? Bit of a history. Perhaps he had knocked Louise up on a previous holiday of hers at the motel and was frightened of losing his job. Couldn't have staff getting intimate with guests, could we? At three months she'd not be showing on this latest visit, but she might have lied to him with a view to getting money out of him for paternity support. No, no joy there, Savage immediately told himself: Jones would only have to request a paternity test, and that'd be the end of Louise's hold over him. In any case, nothing Savage had heard inclined him to believe that Louise was that sort of person. Still, one never knew, and her mother might well have concealed from his colleagues at Pointe Jacques the less savoury aspects of her behaviour. Evidence? None so far. Could Jones have got hold of one of Johnson's scarves, to deflect suspicion? Probably easy enough, even without breaking into the owner's apartment – as the manageress had intimated. And some of the manager's hairs lifted off a hair brush? Could be. But how would Savage ever prove it to a jury? He reconsidered the dossier he had assembled on Jones: brought up in Montreal, lower middle-class family, uneventful school life, no college but had held down perfectly respectable jobs in cafés before his present job on the reception desk. Not known to be dating, but then not every young man has to be dating all the time. The manageress had told him that Jones seemed not to be surprised by the murder: so? A man who watches a lot of TV gets immune to it, he supposed. No, Savage did not believe in the case he was himself building up against Jones. Who, then? He fetched another cup of coffee from the motel coffee shop, determined to think things through and convinced that the crucial clue lay to hand, if only he could dredge it up from the depths of wherever it was.

It suddenly occurred to him that Anna Hayman had made discrete efforts – ever so discrete! - to incriminate Johnson. She had suggested to Crosby that the owner was not trustworthy: 'if what he told me was true', had been her words. She had told Crosby that Johnson was already acquainted with the girl before her arrival. Then, in conversation with himself, she had implied that Johnson was a womaniser. She had explained how easy it was to gain entry to a guest's bedroom, as if she visualised the very encounter. All in all, it looked as if Anna were nudging the police in a particular direction – and the motive for that could only be diverting attention away from her own involvement! Means? What easier for the manageress than to obtain one of the owner's scarves? Opportunity? She had every opportunity. And motive? Sexual frustration, disappointed love. It was obvious, now that he looked at the situation in this new light.

Well, friend, I'm going to cut this story short. Miss Hayman was indicted before a grand jury and found guilty of the murder of Louise Laval. The evidence was circumstantial more than anything else but considered sufficient for a conviction, particularly as no other suspect featured quite so plausibly. Her motive was jealousy that Miss Laval could command Johnson's attentions where she, Anna, could not. She had dressed the murder up to point the finger at Johnson, timing it to coincide with the eve of his departure to an unknown destination, fitting the scene up with his scarf and stray hairs, implying dalliances and shiftiness of character. Unfortunately, despite subtleties, she had overdone it: just too obvious all round once you took in the whole picture. In any case, the chief was anxious to solve the case when there were mutterings in the press about police inefficiency. So the police wrapped up the investigation and boasted of yet another triumph in the battle against crime. Of course, Anna Hayman protested her innocence – but then she would, wouldn't she? Being a sensitive soul, I'm always saddened by miscarriages of justice - but not surprised, in this vale of tears.

There's just one thing I should perhaps add, in case you're still puzzled – a sort of corollary, if you like – just to set the record straight; in the spirit of Christmas – birth of a Saviour and all that. I told you it wasn't an uplifting story, didn't I? Johnson disappeared. It was suspected that he and his friend had perished in the forest at a particularly harsh time of year - if he went trapping with a friend at all and wasn't schmoozing with some dame. But you mustn't believe all you read in the papers. I'm still around.

The Foljambe Blazon
Julius Falconer

Of course, the murder was no surprise – so I was told. The only surprise was that it had not happened earlier. He was unpopular, you see. Rather too much of a bully. Efficient, yes, but on the basis of fear rather than goodwill, and, over his short tenure, he offended virtually all the staff – those that stayed more than a few days, that is. It was only a question of time before someone resented his condescension, brutal put-downs and lack of fellow-feeling and – if you'll pardon a coinage – exited him. Except that that isn't exactly how it was!

This is what happened – and then you'll wish to know, naturally, how I, a lowly parson, became involved. All in good time! The butler, Addiman Mervyn-Cant, known to all as Thomas for short, had been at the Hall for nearly six weeks, having served his apprenticeship (as it were) at Hazlewood Castle. It did not take him long, after his appointment at Steeton, to impose his unlovely regime of below-stairs tyranny, while maintaining a sickening façade of dignity and calm efficiency before his employers, the Foljambes – Sir Francis and his elegant wife Hannah, who let him rule the household without interference because he was efficient.

The house was not full that Christmas Eve - it would take a good many guests to fill it - but there was a healthy complement of visitors to keep the servants busy. Some ten family-members and friends had assembled to join the Foljambes in celebrating the festive season: Lady Foljambe's brother Peter and his new wife; Sir Francis' elderly aunt and her companion; the Hungates from Huddleston House down the road; a nephew of Sir Francis', Roger Landon, and his fiancée, Fleur Vanstone; a widow known to the family as Auntie Ethel; and a retired lawyer, a long-standing friend, called Bertram Ingleby, known to all as Bing. All these guests were known to each other to a greater or lesser degree and were thought to get on, even though some of the relationships required a moderate lubrication.

The calashes and carriages discharged their passengers under the porte-cochère as the snow swirled ever more heavily in the increasing gloom of late afternoon. The guests, hurrying into the entrance-hall, were guided to their rooms by liveried flunkeys to prepare for the start of the festivities. Auntie Ethel needed a little assistance when her stick caught on the edge of a rug and she nearly took a dive into the log-basket. Fortunately Bing was at her elbow to keep her upright and in the process give her waist a playful squeeze. Roger Landon breezed past the waiting flunkeys, with his fiancée on his arm, declaring loudly that he knew which rooms he and Fleur were to occupy and would put no one to trouble to show them the way. Sir Francis gave them a less than approving look but a cordial enough greeting.

Tea would be available at seven o'clock, in the library lobby, while dinner was scheduled for ten o'clock – in the main dining-room, naturally. Otherwise the guests were free to make themselves comfortable in the various other public rooms: the drawing-room, the picture-gallery, the library, the music-room, the smoking-room. Grates everywhere exuded a cheerful warmth. Discreet servants moved quietly here and there to see to guests' wants, maintain the fires and check the rushlights and candles. The sounds of a rising wind percolated only fitfully into the mansion's festive interior.

The cry, when it came, was piercing and prolonged: simultaneously an unmistakeable expression of distress and a summons. The household hastened to the site of it and found Mary, second scullery-maid-once-removed, pointing hysterically, from her vantage-point at the head of the cellar stairs, at the butler's corpse dangling from a meat-hook on the wall. The hook had pierced his neck. A truly gruesome sight. Two footmen, the first and second – or perhaps it was the third and fourth, I forget - hurried forward to lower the body and carry it into the scullery across the passage, where it was laid on the floor and the face covered with the first cloth that came to hand (an apron on a peg, still damp from Mary's recent efforts amongst the pots and pans). The first (or perhaps third) footman then announced with becoming authority (authority accorded him purely on the basis of his physical proximity at the time) that he would apprise Sir Francis of the unfortunate accident – which he did, without being able altogether to exclude a slight hint of satisfaction – and the master of the house soon put in an appearance amongst the frightened servants gathered in a whispering group at the scullery door. Sir Francis inspected the body, shook his head - but whether in sorrow or mystification was uncertain to the bystanders – and asked to see where the body had been found.

'Hm,' he ventured. 'That was rather careless of him. Now we can't keep this from the guests,' he added as he saw that some of them, interrupted in their dressing for dinner, perhaps, or at the card-table, were already in evidence below stairs where they had no right to be, 'but I cannot allow this unfortunate accident to disrupt proceedings more than it need. Find the first footman,' he instructed, turning to his original informant [if he wasn't the first footman], 'and tell him he'll immediately take over the butler's duties. The rest of you proceed as if nothing had happened. The steward will be back shortly, and he'll take care of all needful matters. Right, back to your duties, if you please: there's work to be done, I presume.' Sir Francis was a tall, spare individual with a large nose that would not have shamed an eagle, sleek black hair, a copiously whiskery face (apart from his chin, which was bare) and a slight stoop.

An hour later, not long after tea, the steward, one Samuel Proctor, having run his master to earth in the small drawing-room, craved audience of Sir Francis in private. He coughed hesitantly.

'Sir Francis,' he managed, before stopping dead.

'Yes, man, what is it? This is no time for shilly-shallying. Out with it!'

'Erm, I've inspected the site of the, of the unfortunate business, sir.'

'Yes?'

'And I've come to the conclusion – well, to the conclusion that it wasn't an accident – sir.'

'Not an accident? Of course it was. What are you suggesting, Proctor?'

'Well, sir, when I accompanied the butler – the late butler, that is – down the cellar last, there were four hams hanging from hooks on the wall. Now there are only three.'

'Well, he could hardly catch his throat on a hook if the hook were already occupied by a ham, now, could he?'

'That's my point, Sir Francis. Somebody deliberately removed one of the hams.'

'For tonight's dinner, presumably,' the baronet answered drily. 'Well, if that's all, Proctor, I must get back to my guests.'

'Well, actually, it isn't all, Sir Francis.'

'What, then?'

'An empty meat-hook projects only a little from the wall. No one could walk into it by accident.'

'Are you suggesting – are you suggesting murder, Proctor?'

'Well, Sir Francis.' He coughed. 'What else are we to think?'

'Nonsense! This is a respectable household. Who'd want to murder Thomas, anyway?'

'I don't know, do I, Sir Francis? He could have enemies I know nothing about.'

'This is extremely inconvenient. We can't have disruption on Christmas Eve, with so many guests in the house: it'll have to wait a couple of days, that's all.'

'With respect, Sir Francis, the longer you leave it, the more difficult the affair will be to clear up. The servants will find it difficult to work on in their usual way knowing that there's a murderer in the house who might strike again and no one doing anything about it.'

'Strike again? Great heavens! Oh, very well. Tell the steward from me to ride over to Parlington to see the magistrate – but I can tell you now that Sir Ralph won't be very pleased: I daresay they've got guests too. In fact, I know they have.'

'Thank you, Sir Francis: that'll help settle the servants' worries, knowing there's someone official in charge of the investigation.'

I can tell you, dear reader, that the steward's confidence was riotously misplaced, as, over the years, I had had more than casual dealings with Sir Ralph Gascoigne and his legal activities - non-activities would be more accurate - and could have told Sir Francis for a certainty that the magistrate's response to the alarm would be entirely negligible. In the event, it amounted to no more than a summons to me to make my way as quickly as possible to Steeton Hall to start the investigation. I knew it: I just knew it! Sir Ralph did me the honour of crediting me with success in one or two cases of murder in the district in recent years, but, as always, his felicitations were merely a feint for doing nothing himself. 'You've got the touch, vicar,' he would say. 'You're the man for the job.' Thus shuffling off responsibility on to me, he got on with his hunting, shooting and carousing, oblivious of the criminals in our midst who were *his* responsibility.

Ever conscious of my duty as a man of God – ahem – I apologised to my wife Jane and to the children and promised not to be long (a promise I was unable in the event to keep). The distance to Steeton was less than two miles. I prepared a lanthorn, got my servant Paul to saddle my ancient nag, and off I went, into the dark and the snow. Because of the poor visibility and the uncertain surface below my horse's feet, half-an-hour elapsed before I rode under the ancient gatehouse at the Hall and hammered on the door. As Sir Ralph Gascoigne was expected, I gained immediate entry, but the flunkey's face fell when he saw who it was.

'Ah, tha reverence, it's tha, is it? Ah'm not sure tha's welcome, as we've got a 'ouse full. Couldn't tha make it some other time?'

'Don't be absurd, man,' I expostulated. 'There's been a murder here, and the magistrate has sent me along to look into it.'

"As 'e now?' he asked insolently. 'Ah suppose Ah'd better let tha in. Ah'll tell Sir Francis tha's 'ere – but Ah know 'e was expectin' Sir Ralph in person.'

'Was he?' I snapped crossly. 'Too bad. He's got me instead. I'll wait by the fire so I can warm up a bit.'

Sir Francis appeared shortly afterwards and gave me welcome.

'Rum show, vicar,' he told me, more in surprise, I thought, than in sorrow. 'Murder in the house on Christmas Eve – if it is murder, of course. Goodness me, whatever next? Well, I'll leave you to it, shall I? Shouldn't take you long: can't be many suspects.'

'Where am I to begin?' I asked him uncertainly.

'Wherever you like, your reverence. You'll have a completely free hand.'

'Well, who found the body?'

'One of the maids, I think – but I don't imagine you'll get much out of her, she's that dizzy, by all accounts. Look, wait here, and I'll send the first footman to see you. But make it quick, will you, as he's had to take over the butler's duties and we've got house-guests. This business has put us all behind.' He shuffled off towards the back of the house, leaving me to muse on the vagaries of fate. Some Christmas Eve this was going to be for the vicar of Sherburn! I could hear the noises of the house percolating through: voices, some lowered, some shrill; doors slamming to; comings and goings; music. I imagined that the servants would be in confusion, the guests little out of countenance, the butler's death taking them differently, you understand.

Well, to cut short my doings of the next few moments, I succeeded finally in eliciting from various members of the household all that was known of the sequence of events leading up to the discovery of the body. Thomas had been floating about the place in his usual lofty manner, supervising the preparations, assuring himself that the guests were being attended to, checking that the fires were banked up and so forth. The last person to see him was one of the maidservants, Clara, who was in the laundry when she saw him pass the door in the direction of the cellar. There was nothing unusual about him. His business in the cellar was normal and to be expected. Clara saw no one else.

Of course, I examined the cellar-steps carefully, noting the disposition of the hams, the unevenness of one or two of the steps, the uncertain light even for one with a candle. The meat-hooks were of the kind that hung from a double chain flush with the wall with the hook jutting out from the wall at right angles: quite stout articles, strong enough to carry a carcass, I thought, not just a ham. An accident of the kind that had occurred was unlikely but not inconceivable: except for the fact that a ham had apparently been removed in order to expose the hook. I promised myself that I would keep my mind ajar.

I then made a tour of the outside of the house: no inconsiderable feat in the cold and dark, with the wind flinging snow in my face. My conclusion was that no one had entered the house except by the front door. Between the arrival of the last guests and my own, some snow had fallen. The steward's footprints and mine showed up – just – but no one else's.

I decided that my main recourse must be to the housekeeper, who would be better acquainted with the house below-stairs than anyone else. Mrs Dale, widow (and I was not surprised), with upper arms like tree-trunks and a bust fit, if unsupported, to put her flat on her face, was the epitome of housekeepership (perhaps that should be 'housekeeperhood': no matter) and clearly resented the time she had to give to answering my questions. Her opinion of the late butler was candid and sour. She granted that he was efficient, suitably deferential to his employers without being sycophantic, and neither pompous nor pretentious. However, she noted that he simply was not popular with the staff: too dour, inflexible, in a way despotic (even though it was in the interests of efficiency). Furthermore, she had more than once noticed his eye roving amongst the maidservants, which unsettled them. I asked whether she had any suspicions as to who might have wished him ill.

'Ill? Everyone!'

'Ah, but to the point of murder?'

'Well, no, but 'ow do Ah know whether 'e 'adn't pushed a girl too 'ard and lived - or rather died – to regret it?' Her voice suddenly dropped. 'Could 'ave got one – well, tha knows, vicar.' I ignored the innuendo.

'But wouldn't it take a *man* to murder him with a meat-hook?'

'Mebbe.' I took a look at her shoulders and doubted the truth of my own question.

'No recent quarrels or rows that you know of?'

'No more nor usual. Any 'ouse'old 'as its share o' rows, Ah daresay: even tha's, Ah've no doubt.' She glared at me over her several chins.

'And how did you get on with him personally?' She pulled herself up.

'A professional relationship, 'im in 'is job, me in mine. We knew where we stood. 'Ere, tha's not suggestin' – '

'No, no, Mistress Dale,' I said hastily. 'Merely asking round.' I lowered my voice. 'Could any of the manservants have wanted his job?'

'We're Christians 'ere, vicar, so put that idea out o' tha 'ead.'

'Well, I daresay we are, mistress, but somebody wanted him out of the way. You can't deny that.'

'Not one of us.' She lowered her voice as I had done earlier. 'Try t'guests.'

'Oh, no, I don't think so: what would they be doing half-way down the cellar-steps?'

'Murdering t'butler.'

'Well, thank you, mistress, you've been most helpful. So sorry to have taken up your time.'

I sidled out of the kitchen and all but bumped into a maidservant who might, for all I knew, have been listening intently to our conversation.

'Ah, young woman,' I hailed her, 'you wouldn't be kind enough to show me Thomas' room, would you?'

'No, sir, can't, sir, don't know where it is, sir.' I sighed. Of course, if I had thought, I should have realised that, more probably than not, the male staff and the female staff occupied rooms in different parts of the house, or at least at different ends of the same corridor. I collared a manservant and put my question. He nodded, led me up the back stairs to the top floor and, with a slight obeisance but no words, indicated a door along the servants' corridor. I went in. The room was orderly: two single beds, a wash-basin, a vanity table, a wardrobe, a polished wooden floor with a rug between the beds, a small window giving on to the front lawn; nothing out of place. I did not know what I expected to find; I knew I was playing for time, hoping that something unusual would strike me. It did; and didn't. I searched the room, not thoroughly, but randomly, not knowing precisely what I was looking for. In the wardrobe were a few letters, some broadside ballads, a handful of pamphlets on various subjects (plays, a bit of poetry, a copy of the Albany Almanack), a Bible and a scrap of paper bearing the following words:

Sa. on a bend between six escallops or an inescutcheon argent.

There was more, but I had no chance to read it. I had got to the end of the first line, when all went black and I saw stars (can't rightly remember in which order those two events occurred). As I realised later, someone had entered the room while I was engrossed in my search and knocked me on the head. What an indignity for the vicar of Sherburn! So unexpected, too!

When I recovered consciousness, quite ignorant of how long I had been unaware of my surroundings, I felt the lump on my head, dragged myself to my feet using the bed for support and tried to remember where I was and what I had been doing. Slowly memory returned. Yes, I was investigating a murder (I was now convinced it was murder). The butler's. At Steeton Hall. On Christmas Eve 1729. I had been searching the murdered man's room when I was interrupted in my perusal of the documents in his wardrobe. I tried in vain to remember the document I had been reading when some villain had taken me by surprise. The details continued to elude me, but I became sure it had been a blazon. Didn't scallops feature? I thought so. I could not for the life of me, however, remember any more or work out its relevance to my investigation or why it had – as I discovered – disappeared, presumably into the pocket of my aggressor. A mystery. Another mystery was the whereabouts of my wig! The villain must have carried it off: a pox on him.

At length, realising that the butler's room had yielded all its secrets, such as they were, I made to return downstairs and seek something restorative before continuing my work. The door was locked! I muttered some mild imprecations, valiantly restraining myself in honour of the season, and began to bang on the door. No one answered. The servants were presumably engaged downstairs, and I was two floors up in the roof, out of sight, out of hearing and out of mind. Was ever a vicar so circumstanced?

Time passed - how much time I am uncertain: perhaps an hour? - before my noisy alert was answered and the door opened. It was one of the footmen who was as astonished to see me as I was relieved to see him.

'Your reverence,' he stammered, 'what, what on earth art tha doin' 'ere?'

'That's what I'd like to know,' I replied. 'But never mind that: I must get back downstairs.'

'Art tha goin' to look for t'first footman as well?'

'As well as what?'

'As well as everybody else: 'e's disappeared, tha knows.'

'What? What do you mean, "disappeared"?'

'Vanished! 'E told one o' t' footmen that 'e were goin' to check t'fire in t'small drawin'-room, but 'e never arrived. Leastways, the fire went out.'

'My goodness me, there's no time to waste. Here, let me past.'

I hurried down two flights of stairs, passing no one on the way, but saw no evidence to support the manservant's news that 'everyone' was looking for the first footman. On the contrary, the house seemed singularly well-ordered; bustling but calm. Asking various people where I might find Sir Francis, I tracked him down eventually in the music-room enjoying a game of cards with Bing and the Hungates.

'Sir Francis,' I began peremptorily, without waiting for a suitable pause in the game.

'Reverend, reverend,' interrupted Sir Francis, unperturbed. 'Calm yourself.'

'But this is an emergency,' I insisted.

'You mean the murder? All solved, I'm glad to say.'

'Solved?!'

'Oh, yes. So sorry you've been troubled. Solved itself, really. Now, if you'll forgive us - '

'But who by? How?'

'Look, your reverence, can't you see we're engaged?'

'But I shall have to give an account of myself to Sir Ralph Gascoigne. What am I to tell him: that I got locked in a bedroom, missed the fun, lost my wig and contributed nothing to the solution of a dastardly crime?'

'Let me just tell you what happened, then you can go your way with a peaceful conscience. How would that be? Actually, you can take some of the credit, you know. When the first footman – he's the murderer, by the way – got wind of your investigation and realised you were hot on his trail – well, I exaggerate a little, perhaps, but we'll let that pass – he absconded; did a bunk; fled. He won't survive in this weather: he'll come crawling back to take his medicine. Even if he doesn't, it won't be long before he's picked up. So, your reverence - '

'But why did he kill the butler?'

'Who knows? I suspect Thomas was bullying him, and he'd had enough.'

'And how do you know he's the murderer?'

'It's obvious. Why else would he cut and run? But I'm not going to bother my head about the matter any further, and I advise you to do the same.'

'But I sustained an injury. Got locked in a room. And I've been humiliated.'

'If you're referring to the, er, lack of headwear you mentioned, I'm sure the housekeeper can find something to, er, you know, disguise your, well, er, your, well, let's not mince our words, vicar - your baldness. So think no more about it, your reverence – and thanks for your time. Happy Christmas to your family, by the way.'

I understood that I was dismissed. Was I simply to return home: is that what Sir Francis expected? I sat in the main hall, close to the fire, and cogitated. The story that Sir Francis had spun me lacked coherence: he may have been taken in by it, but I wasn't. Firstly, by no stretch of the imagination could I be said to have been hot on the murderer's trail: I was nowhere near it! Secondly, why should the first footman have followed me up to the butler's room and assaulted me – me, a clergyman! – with the sole aim, apparently, of appropriating a small piece of paper containing (if I was right) a blazon? Walking off with my wig was uncalled for; the only reason for it that occurred to me was sheer devilry. Thirdly, had any search been made for the missing murderer: might he not still be on the premises, plotting further mischief? Sir Francis' attitude was all too facile: keener on entertaining his guests than pursuing the cause of justice. In the light of these cogitations, I determined to prowl further and shed more light, if I could. I cast a small prayer heavenward.

The next thing was to apply to the housekeeper for a wig to cover my nakedness. I found her eventually in the larder inspecting her plum puddings, and she acquiesced readily to my request.

'Sir Francis won't mind tha 'avin' an old one of 'is,' she told me robustly. 'Bit moth-eaten; maybe a bit large; but then it's not for long, is it?' Clearly word had got round that my services at the

Hall were no longer needed! Sir Francis might not have minded about his wig: but what about me?! I decided to question Mistress Dale again in the light of Sir Francis' accusation. If the first footman's flight was common knowledge, I should not be guilty of an indiscretion.

'Tell me, mistress,' I ventured before she could dash off to another chore, 'had Thomas been bullying the first footman more than usual lately, do you know? Could that account for matters?'

'Don't rightly know, do Ah? Ma job's 'ousekeepin', not runnin' after footmen! Low form of life, really; and if 'e couldn't look after 'isself, well, a poor specimen, Ah say.'

'But was he a poor specimen?'

'That's enough o' that, tha reverence. Ah've no time to be gossipin'.'

By this time, I could see dishes being carried out to the dining-room: pigeon, venison, roast beef, something I took to be duck (unless it was unusually plump partridge), vegetables, sauces – in a word, the full works. And here was I, neither family, guest nor servant and likely to go without sustenance as a consequence!

The dining-room at Steeton was a gracious room, with a stone moulded fireplace, a Yorkshire stone floor, mullioned windows (as I discovered later) and a superb vaulted stone-beamed ceiling. The guests, as I could see when I peered through the door and risked the just wrath of servants scurrying hither and thither, were all seated at a massive table nearly the length of the room, the host and hostess at the head and foot respectively and six guests down each side. Conversation flowed freely – until the catastrophe! Then there were just gasps, of surprise from the men and of horror from the women. What happened was this. One of the servants moved too close to the window, jogged the curtain and dislodged the body of the first footman that had been concealed behind it. The body fell into the room and coiled into a heap on the floor behind Fleur Vanstone. She screamed loudly, piercingly, amid the gasps, rose to her feet in agitation, upset the gravy-bowl which in turn cannoned into the table centre-piece, a carefully poised porcelain figure of – well, delicacy forbids my mentioning the subject of the statue – which crashed head-first on to the table and shattered. Havoc ensued, as the women rushed to the exit hampered by the men in a dither. The servants lost control of their trays, glasses of wine toppled and spilt, chairs tipped over. The body lay unmindful of the chaos. I stepped forward, believing it to be incumbent on me, as, so to speak, Sir Ralph Gascoigne's deputy, to intervene. Sir Francis seeming too dazed to be of much service, I asked two male servants to be kind enough to remove the body upstairs to its bedroom and then I hoped we could return the house to some sort of normality. I explained to the hosts that since, in my opinion, nothing was to be gained by abandoning the meal, going into mourning, evacuating the house (as if one could in a blizzard!) or clapping everyone in irons, the party should resume their seats at table as soon as the servants had restored order amongst the cutlery and crockery and the ladies had had a chance to recover from their experience.

You can imagine that what passes in polite company for my mind was racing away in speculation. The chances of the first footman's being still cast as the butler's murderer were dimming – unless we had two murderers in the house. Great heavens! The plot was increasing in complexity with every moment that passed. While the meal continued, I decided to interview some of the guests in private, inviting them to join me one by one in the hall. I say 'some' advisedly, as I could not really see Auntie Ethel or Sir Francis' elderly aunt (for example) attaching the butler to a meat-hook on the cellar-steps or manhandling a corpse into the dining-room alcove without being noticed. This left the following: nephew Roger, brother Peter, neighbour Mr Hungate, retired lawyer Bertram Ingleby ('Bing'), Sir Francis himself and, amongst the women, the two younger wives (Roger's and Peter's).

However, securing permission from Sir Francis, who had by this time recovered his usual poise and was again seated at the head of the table offering his guests hospitality, for the procedure I had in mind proved more difficult than I imagined. He seemed rather to object to my continuing presence at the Hall.

'There's nothing more you can do here, vicar,' he told me brusquely. 'Go home. Oh, I see: it's the snow that's keeping you, is it? Lady Foljambe will see you accommodated. Hannah, would you be kind enough to organise a room for the reverend?' he said loudly down the table. 'So, goodnight, vicar, and sweet dreams.' I continued to keep my voice low.

'Well, no, Sir Francis,' I answered him, 'I don't think Sir Ralph would be happy for me to abandon my post at this stage. Furthermore, time is valuable, you know, and we don't want another murder on our hands, do we?'

'Yes, but what can you do, honestly? You've tried, and no one can ask more than that of a man. Don't worry, I'll get Sir Ralph himself over in the morning, so that you can get back to your family. Oh, I forgot, you're spending the night here. Well, as I say - '

'All I want to do is to have a word with everyone, to see whether anything unusual was noticed.'

'Absolutely no need, vicar. You've done what you can, and we're grateful. Sleep tight.'

'But nobody will sleep peacefully tonight thinking there might be a murderer at large.' I assured Sir Francis that my purpose was not to level accusations at his guests but to seek information, however seemingly trivial. On the other hand, bearing in mind the housekeeper's caveat that the murderer was to be sought amongst the guests rather than amongst the servants, I thought I should frame my questions accordingly! Seeing the reaction of the two guests within earshot of my request, Sir Francis finally acquiesced.

Well, to spare you, patient reader, the full account of my interviews, I can tell you that I discovered nothing untoward. I questioned the 'suspects' on their movements, impressions and suspicions: nothing. Various possibilities could account for this state of affairs (I told myself): the people I interviewed were adroit liars; I was particularly dense and insensitive; I was being told the strict truth; the whole thing was a dream played out in my head as I lay on the floor of the butler's bedroom. I even took the precaution of once again walking round the outside of the Hall to

An Anthology of Christmas Murders

see whether footsteps in the snow might betray the presence of an intruder who had fled the gathering after perpetrating the dastardly act. I quickly realised that the ever more abundant snow would have obliterated any traces. Before interviewing the servants, I asked one of them in which room the body had been laid and went up to carry out a search. There was no sign of the scrap of paper containing (as I thought) a blazon. Perhaps he had got rid of it, deeming it damning evidence; perhaps he never had it; perhaps I was losing my marbles – all possibilities. I carefully observed the manner of his death: he had been stabbed in the back, presumably in the dining-room when he had his back to the curtain, behind which the murderer had hidden, with a knife the blade of which measured, say, half-an-inch in width: a kitchen-knife, perhaps, or a small trade-knife. Anyone would have had easy access to a suitable weapon, perhaps needing to reach for it no further than his own belt. No satisfaction there, then.

Having thus succeeded in gaining absolutely nothing, and seeing from Sir Francis' long-case clock in the hall that midnight was but a few minutes away, I determined to put all my effort into the only real clue I had: the missing blazon. I tried to recapture the few words I had been able to digest before being knocked on the sconce. I was sure scallops came into it somewhere. I was also sure that my firm impression at the time was that I was reading a blazon. I am not, heaven knows, learned in heraldic lore (or indeed in much else), but I knew a little about the language of achievements and the way of setting out the details of a coat of arms, starting with the shield, going on to the crest and then the mantling, the supporters and finally the motto. Through the fog I thought further that the first letters I read were 'sa.', which would mean sable, the colour of the shield in the arms being described. Apart from the vaguest further memory of something bent, the rest was irrecoverable. The paper on which the words were written was obviously important: the more I considered the matter, the more convinced I became that I had been prevented from reading the piece of paper with a blow to the head, from which I was lucky to have recovered with so little damage to my cerebral workings, and that my assailant had wrenched it from my grasp and gone off

41

with it because it was in some way incriminating. I could not begin to imagine how. Or perhaps it was not the blazon itself: perhaps it was the handwriting, or what succeeded the blazon, or the verso.

I sought out Sir Francis as being the one most likely to shed light on the mystery. He was seated at the dining-room table with the other men of the party, the ladies having withdrawn. I begged the favour of a few words.

'What is it now, vicar?' he asked me with evident irritation.

'It may be important, Sir Francis.'

'May it? Oh, very well.' He rose ungraciously and showed me out into the hall. 'But make it quick, will you?' Having outlined the circumstances of my search of the butler's room, I explained my concern about the missing sheet of paper.

'I'm sure it was a blazon, Sir Francis. Something about some scallops on black, if I remember correctly. And I can't find it either on the first footman's person or in his room.'

'No mystery there, surely, vicar? It's undoubtedly the blazon of our Foljambe coat of arms.'

'Is it? How does it go?'

'Not sure in detail, but you can see the arms themselves in the library.'

'Ah. But why would the butler have the blazon amongst his papers? And why should someone try to stop me reading it?'

'Imagination, sheer imagination! And why shouldn't the butler have it in his room? He lives and works here. No doubt proud to be employed by the Foljambes. A distinguished family, you know, vicar: ancient lineage, notable members, imposing family mansion – and I don't mean this place: we're merely cadets here – a coat of arms, deeds of derring-do: more than enough to constitute important gentry. Go back to the Normans, you know. Sir Henry accompanied Richard I on his crusade. Then there was Sir Godfrey, squire to both Henry VII and Henry VIII. We should also mention - ' He coughed. 'Sorry, this is no time to be rambling on about how important we are. What was it you wanted? I've forgotten.'

'More details of the blazon,' I restricted myself to replying.

'Ah, yes. Well, follow me, vicar.' Clearly, a reminder of the illustriousness of his family had galvanised him into an action that would spread its fame even into the modest vicarage at Sherburn. We trooped (if two can 'troop') along to the library – a long, low room to the north of the house, containing what I considered rather a modest collection of books: the Foljambes were probably more adept at exercising their hunting-crops than their intellects. He rummaged around for a suitable volume, riffled through it and proudly pointed to a full achievement with, underneath it, the following blazon:

> Sa., on a bend between six escallops or an inescutcheon argent charged with a lion rampant azure. *Crest*: On a wreath a man's leg or jambe, couped at the thigh, armed and spurred, quarterly or and sa. *Additional crests granted by Henry VIII.:* 1. On a chapeau gu., turned up erm., a tiger statant arg., ducally gorged or. 2. On a wreath a calopus or chat-loup passant: quarterly or and sa., horned also quarterly of the same. *Supporters*: Dexter, an antelope quarterly or and sa.; sinister, a tiger arg. ducally gorged or*.

English of sorts. Except for the French bits, of course. The entry confirmed me in my view that what I had fleetingly seen in the butler's room was indeed a description of the Foljambe arms. What then?

'Handsome, don't you think, vicar?' the baronet interrupted my thoughts.

'Yes, indeed,' I agreed, without having considered the matter. If only I could find that piece of paper! 'What's it got to do with the murders, I wonder,' I said out loud.

'It's only you saying that, vicar. You're being fanciful. Go to bed, and I'll get old Gascoigne in tomorrow. Don't bother your head about the matter any longer. Now I think of it, perhaps the

---

*In plain English: A black shield crossed by a yellow (gold) band with three scallop-shells on either side. At the top of the band, a blue rampant lion on a small silver shield. Crest: a man's leg cut off at the thigh, in armour and spurs, on a wreath, both leg and wreath striped gold and black. Additional crests granted by Henry VIII: 1. On a red hat with an ermine brim, a standing tiger, with a coronet round its throat. 2. On a wreath, a calopus or wolf-cat, walking, with a golden coronet round its throat. Supporters: on the right, an antelope striped gold and black; on the left, a silver tiger with a golden coronet round its throat.

magistrate was being a little optimistic in imagining you could do anything here – just being his usual lazy self, I suppose, and, er, overestimating your, er, powers of detection. Well, goodnight, vicar. I suppose Hannah has fixed you up with a room for the night?' I went away not to go to bed but to think.

And how I thought! My hunger lent wings to my imagination, and I cogitated as I had not cogitated for a long time – not for three months, in fact, since I reasoned my way to – or, if you prefer, stumbled on - the answer to the riddle of the Elmete agitators. I had retired to a dimly lit corner of the entrance-hall, within sight of the hearth, and made myself comfortable in a tapestried wing-chair that happened to be lurking there. I snuggled back, folded my hands in my lap, closed my eyes and set about thinking my way through the evening, sifting through all I had heard, seen and experienced in the last hours. The salient facts which I eventually assembled were four in number, and together they amounted to a case which was unexpected and unsavoury but, I was convinced, none the less sure for that. They were:

1. My interviews with the guests and servants had yielded nothing.

2. The baronet was strikingly nonchalant for one who had given house-room to two murders in the space of an evening.

3. He seemed excessively keen to dismiss my questions and get rid of me, on the plea largely of my incompetence. Only the blizzard had prevented him from turning me out of doors long since.

4. The blazon was significant, whatever he might say to the contrary; and part of its wording particularly so.

One mystery remained – a significant one – but I thought I might guess at it. It would not upset the essential pattern of my reconstruction. The author of the two murders and of my bump on the sconce was Sir Francis Foljambe himself! This is how I saw things. The baronet invited the butler into the cellar on some pretext or other, casually removed the meat-hook from the wall, having previously disposed of its ham, suddenly skewered the butler with it and hoisted the hook back on the wall, with the hapless victim still attached to it. So far so good. The crime could not, however, remain long concealed, once the steward had waved the word 'murder' around, and Sir Francis was obliged to call on the services of the magistrate, knowing full well that the latter was most unlikely to bestir himself on a snowy Christmas Eve! His ad hoc deputy was likely to be – and was! – that buffoon, the incompetent vicar of Sherburn: yours truly! As I bumbled my way through my investigation, Sir Francis realised that he had not properly considered the possible presence of incriminating evidence in the butler's room but, making his hasty way there, surprised me already in possession of the premises. A knock on the head (*my* head!) gave him time to riffle through the butler's few books and papers and remove what he considered incriminating. It so happened that I noticed the theft of one paper in particular, the Foljambe blazon. There could have been others.

However, his exit from the butler's room, my wig in hand (I suspect), and his locking of the door behind him were witnessed by the first footman. The latter had to be eliminated, as either Sir Francis saw him or he approached Sir Francis with an accusation. It was one thing for the master of the house to be seen, as perhaps he was, in the vicinity of the cellar in his own house, quite another to be emerging from a room on the upper floor whence the prisoner would soon be knocking a tattoo in his bid for freedom. Sir Francis therefore skulked around awaiting a suitable opportunity to dispose of the first footman. His opportunity arose in the dining-room, and, on such a night, the only hiding-place for the corpse that presented itself at short notice was the very convenient alcove behind the curtains; he might hope to remove and dispose of the body more securely at some later hour. It was his misfortune, although not yet fatal, for the body to be discovered by accident: the circumstance lent added urgency to the hunt for the, or for a second, killer.

I looked for the motive of the butler's murder in the missing blazon, as that was the precise document which the murderer had appropriated. One phrase in particular, as I said, attracted my attention: 'ducally gorged'. As I understood the terminology, this had nothing to do with ducal status but meant simply that, by way of pure decoration, the animal wore a coronet round its throat (or 'gorge'). This suggested to me that the butler had designs on the Foljambe coat of arms, that is, on the baronetcy or estate(s) or Hall - or no doubt all three at once, as a package. Was he an illegitimate member of the family? had he some other hold on Sir Francis, such as knowledge of the latter's usurpation of the title? I was not destined to find out. Whatever of that, it suggested to Sir Francis the manner of the butler's death, by way of a fatal irony.

Although sure of my conclusions – well, pretty sure, in so far as certainty about anything is possible in this vale of tears and travail - I was unsure how to act on them in accordance with the canons of citizenship, justice and propriety. Eventually I decided to tax Sir Francis with them and challenge him to give himself up to the authorities – if I was right in my surmise. On the basis of this resolution, I rose from my chair and went in search of my quarry, only to find that no one seemed to know where he was. My insistence caused no little agitation in a household already shaken by two murders, and a full-scale search was instituted. He was found eventually in his bedroom, supine, lifeless, clutching his chest, with a final rictus of pain distorting his aristocratic features: struck down by an Unknown Hand – except that, of course, gentle reader, you and I, God-fearers both, know Whose Hand it was! *Miserere Deus.*

Murders don't stop even at Christmas
Peter Good

If you were to travel from the State of Zimpopo to the State of Zambanyika in Central Africa, you would likely travel down Highway 27, passing through the district town of Legion: the last town before the border crossing over the Shumva River. On arriving in Legion, such serene visions would meet your eyes that you could be forgiven for thinking you had reached the epitome of an idyllic district township: broad spotlessly clean streets; lovely decorated shops set amongst perfectly mown lawns; and mature trees between almost all the buildings; at the centre a dam, where the town's inhabitants rest on white-painted park benches under the shade of the huge trunks of the massive boabab trees, while their children feed the ducks and swans. Yes, it is easy to understand why so many people, on reaching retirement age, choose to settle here in the town of Legion.

But things are never as they seem, and this was the case on Christmas Day, 2006, when the town was shocked to its core by the brutal killing of two of its most beloved residents: a deed so horrible that it had folk locking their doors and looking over their shoulders wondering who in their midst could possibly be capable of committing such a foul deed. Heaven forbid that it might be a member of their own community!

Ben Van Vuuren had been in the police force for twelve years and had loved every single day of that time doing what he enjoyed most: being a district policeman. A district policeman is usually stationed at a police station far out from the nearest big city and consequently has to investigate anything and everything, from the simple theft of a chicken to a murder, seeing it through to conclusion, be it at the local court or at a high court in the nearest city. It was this variety that Ben loved so much. He held the rank of inspector at the Legion Police Station in the town of Legion in the southern part of Zimpopo that bordered on to Zambanyika. Ben was in charge and was supported by two constables: Ian 'Chalky' White and David Hardy. Together they staffed the police station. Then there was the 'African' contingent, with its twenty African constables headed by Sergeant Major Mpofu. The police station itself consisted of an office for the member in charge, in this case Ben, and the charge office staffed by the two European constables: White and Hardy. The charge office also contained the SSB Radio, which they relied on for messages to and from their police headquarters some 100 miles to the north of them in Bulawadi, affectionately known to all as Bullys. Then there was an office for the use of Sergeant Major Mpofu, and lastly an office in which the African constables congregated.

In the police camp, there was a house for the member in charge, a police mess wherein lived the two European constables, a house for the sergeant major and a further twelve houses. Of these, the eight larger ones were for the eight married African constables, and the remaining four smaller ones, which could have comfortably housed three occupants each, accounted for the twelve single African constables.

Legion Town was then, as indeed it is now, a small and close-knit settlement. It had one large shop - Legion Supermarket - which had a butchery, bakery, general goods, liquor store and a clothing section all under one roof. It was owned and run by Uyz (pronounced Ace) Dupree and his wife Matilda, a local African woman whom he had married some forty years ago. Uyz was a short squat man, bald, but sporting a well-trimmed beard and possessing a tanned skin acquired through having lived in Africa his entire life. Matilda, too, was short and plump. Both were as gentle as could be, always with a ready smile and happy to assist anyone. It was a well-known fact that they frequently provided goods on credit to the less fortunate. They had one child: a daughter named Jessica. She was a slim and beautiful girl aged twenty-three, who also worked in the supermarket. Jessica was currently dating two men: Joseph Swanson and James Johansson.

Opposite the superstore stood the town's only bank: the Zimpopo National Bank, or ZIMNAT Bank, as it was known. Its manager, Brian Moody, was a tall man in his fifties, with piercing grey-green eyes - a feature which put off many a person from their original purpose when going in to ask for a loan! Married for some twenty years, Brian and his wife Anne remained childless for no reason other than that they had both agreed they did not want children.

Then there was the post office, run by Tim and Audrey Smith, a couple in their sixties, born and bred in Legion. Within the post office was the telephone exchange, manned for the past eight years by twenty-eight-year-old Brandie Thompson.

Mary Hartley was the owner of Mary's Motel, the last 'stopping-off' place for travellers proceeding south to Zambanyika. Mary was a polite, well-rounded and jolly woman with a lovely warm smile, always ready to chat and joke with one and all. Her kitchen was renowned for serving up the most delicious meals, and thus nearly all the local inhabitants at one time or another frequented the dining-room.

The town hall was situated in the town centre on the east side of the dam. Mayor Bill Owens was a portly, well-liked and respected man who had held office for two terms now and was likely to be re-elected for many more. He and his wife June had been happily married for thirty-five years.

Two miles to the west of the town stood both the Salvation Army Mission and the hospital. The Mission was overseen by Major Dunn: a generous woman with a winning smile who went out of her way to help all, especially the local Africans. Senior Nurse Anthea Woodley, Inspector Ben Van Vuuren's girlfriend at the time, ran the hospital.

There were three major cattle ranches in the area. The largest, Bar 8, was owned and run by Bill Swanson: a Bulawadi-born man who had lived all his life in Zimpopo. His parents had built the ranch in the early 1900s, running it until their deaths in the 1960s, when Bill took over ownership shortly after he and his wife Betty had married. Bill and Betty had one son, Joseph, who, having been raised on the ranch, had ranching in his blood. On turning twenty-one, he went into partnership with his father on the ranch.

Tokwe Ranch was a little smaller than Bar 8. It was owned and run by Ewen Van Der Merwe, together with his wife Sandra. They were both born in Zambanyika, but came to Zimpopo in 1959 and purchased the land on which the ranch now stood. They had only one child, their daughter Irene, who worked at Mary's Motel as a receptionist.

The smallest of the three ranches was Lazy J. In 1959, Joshua and Jillian Johansson had come to Zimpopo and purchased the land on which Lazy J now stood, running it as a ranch ever since. James, the eldest of their two children, assisted his parents in its running, though if the truth be told he was as lazy as his father with virtually all the work being left to Nduna, their African foreman. Lazy J: the locals giggled at the name, thinking it very apt in the circumstances! Jenny, James' sister, had nothing to do with the ranch and worked at the Legion Supermarket.

Apart from the Duprees, who had a house built on to their supermarket, the town's residents had homes on the eastern side of the dam behind the town hall. Situated in the forested area that surrounded Legion Town, each home had approximately an acre of land, all of which contributed to the idyll that was Legion Town, until that fateful Christmas Day in the year 2006 - which would remain in the minds of all the town's inhabitants for years to come!

On Christmas morning, Jenny Johansson was woken by knocking at her door. She glanced over at her alarm-clock: it was 7 a.m.

'Who on earth is knocking at this time of the morning - and on this day of all days?' she mused, before sitting up and calling,

'Come in!' The door opened, and in stepped her brother James. 'James!' she exclaimed. 'What do you want so early? I was enjoying a nice lie-in for once.' And she stared at her brother, waiting for his response. James broke into a wide grin.

'I thought you would like to come with me to Legion Town. We could go and wish all those who weren't at Mary's Motel last night a Merry Christmas.' He looked back at her still smiling, waiting to hear her reply.

'At this time of the morning?' she queried.

'Well, by the time you get up, get changed, and we drive into Legion, it'll be about 8.30, and most of the town's inhabitants will be awake by then. Come on, sis, it will be good fun! We might even get a drink and some mince-pies or Christmas cake.' He tailed off as Jenny looked back at him. She knew there were some that were not at the party last night, and, yes, it would be nice to go and see them and wish them a Merry Christmas.

'Oh, OK, now go on get out so I can get up and dressed. I'll meet you in the lounge in a moment or two.'

Smiling, James left her room, closing the door behind him as he strolled down to the lounge and walked over to the window. He stood there, looking out at nothing in particular, just watching the sun, which had been up since 6 a.m. and was already beating down on the earth. No doubt the temperature would soon be rising; people, as usual, would be happy to be inside, or under shady trees, as the heat rose. He had been there just twenty minutes when his sister walked in.

'Right, I'm ready, let's go!' she said cheerfully.

James turned, smiled at her and led the way out to his white Ford pick-up truck. Opening the driver's door, he jumped in, closing it behind him as Jenny opened the other door and gracefully eased herself into the passenger seat. James fired up the motor, and the engine barked into life. Engaging gear, James drove out from the ranch-house and down the dirt road that led from the ranch towards the main road - Highway 27 - which ran from Zimpopo to Zambanyika in the south. They rumbled over several cattle-grids, placed there to stop cattle from straying, past locked gates and barbed-wire fences trailing out from each side of the road into the ranch land. After some five miles of dirt road, they crossed the final cattle-grid, and, once over that, they were on to Highway 27. Turning left, James drove northwards towards Legion Town. It was 8.45 a.m. when they arrived in Legion Town.

'Let's do our first call on the Duprees,' said James. Without waiting for a response from his sister, he turned up a side road and headed to the house that was built on to the Legion Supermarket. He pulled to a stop outside a small neat garden with white picket fence in front of the main door to the Duprees' house. He switched off the engine, pulled up the brake lever and, opening his door, said, 'Come on, sis!' Jenny got out, joining her brother as he opened the gate. They walked up to the door together.

James stuck out his right hand to give the door a knock, but, as his hand came into contact with the door, it slowly swung open.

'That's strange,' Jenny said.

'Yeah,' replied James. 'I know people tend not to lock their doors, but not many leave them open!' Cautiously, he put out his left hand to stop his sister going in. 'Let's be careful,' he said. 'I mean, maybe they've gone away and that's the reason they weren't at the party. Who knows who might have opened this door?' He paused, and Jenny quickly reached into her pocket for her mobile phone.

'Should we not call the police?' she asked, adding, with a sense of fear in her voice, 'What if someone is inside, maybe a burglar?'

'Well, not yet,' James quickly replied. 'Tell you what, you stay here by the door, and I'll go in and take a quick look around.' And with that he slowly walked into the house, leaving his sister at the doorway. A few moments later Jenny heard her brother cry out.

'Jenny, use your phone to call the police. They're both in here - DEAD!' Jenny let out a gasp and then quickly dialled the police station.

Constable David Hardy had drawn the short straw: he was the one unfortunate enough to have been selected for duty on Christmas Day. He was sitting in the charge office reading a book when the telephone rang. Putting down his book, he picked up the phone.

'Legion Police Constable Hardy speaking. How can I help you?'

'It's Jenny Johansson,' shouted the caller frantically. 'I'm at the Legion Supermarket, with my brother … the door to the Duprees' home was open … my brother went in … the Duprees: they're both dead!' she blurted. Constable Hardy, shaken by what he had just heard, replied:

'Ask your brother to come out straight away and join you by the door. We'll be there as soon as possible.' On getting her assent, he hung up and immediately dialled his member-in-charge. The phone rang a few times before it was answered.

'Hello, Ben Van Vuuren.' Constable Hardy quickly rattled off details of the call he had just received.

'Constable Hardy, please get Constable White, Sergeant Major Mpofu and four of the African constables,' instructed Inspector Van Vuuren. 'I'll be over as soon as I can,' and he hung up, muttering to himself, 'Murders don't stop even at Christmas!'

Constable Hardy did just as the inspector had instructed, and soon all those whom he called were with him at the charge office, each very disturbed by the devastating news of the Duprees' deaths - though at this stage, of course, it was not known whether their deaths were from natural causes or whether it was murder. A few minutes passed, and Inspector Van Vuuren appeared in uniform. He asked Constable White and Sergeant Major Mpofu to accompany him in the Chevrolet police car to the Duprees' home at the Legion Supermarket. The others were to follow in the police Landrover.

On arrival, they alighted from their respective vehicles, Inspector Van Vuuren giving instructions. Some were to go to the rear door of the house, tape it off and stand watch. Sergeant Major Mpofu and Constable Hardy would tape off the front. Constable White was to accompany Jenny Johansson, who was by the front door with her brother, sobbing quite uncontrollably, over to the motel, where he could attempt to calm her with a cup of tea. The inspector would question James.

'Can you describe the events that led you here and how you came to find the Duprees?' he asked James.

'Well, I woke my sister Jenny up this morning and suggested we come over and wish the Duprees a Happy Christmas, as they were not at the motel party last night,' began James. He then continued to relate what had happened. He told Inspector Van Vuuren about the open door and how he had gone inside leaving his sister outside, before going on to describe how he had found Mrs Dupree on the floor, next to the bread stall. 'I leant over and felt the side of her neck for a pulse and found none and saw that she didn't appear to be breathing.' He paused for a moment, then continued: 'I then stepped over her body, went towards the door that led from the store into their house, and there, in the doorway, was Mr Dupree, lying in a pool of blood, and I could tell right away that he too wasn't breathing. That's when I called out to my sister to phone you ... and I guess that's all I know,' he concluded. Inspector Ben Van Vuuren, who had taken a course in shorthand, wrote down all that James Johansson told him.

'Thanks, I suggest you go and join your sister and Constable White at the motel,' he said, as he closed his notebook.

As James departed, Inspector Van Vuuren, Sergeant Major Mpofu and Constable Hardy donned rubber gloves and went slowly into the supermarket. They proceeded up the aisle past the tools' section and on to the bread stall, where they came on the body of Mrs Dupree. She was lying on her stomach, arms above her head. Inspector Van Vuuren bent down and on examination discovered that she appeared to have been struck on the head, the blood matting her hair. Constable Hardy photographed the scene whilst Van Vuuren and Mpofu continued slowly towards the doorway that led from the supermarket to the house. On the floor in front of the door lay the crumpled body of Mr Dupree. He was lying on his back with one leg folded beneath him. He too suffered several heavy blows to the front of his head, which had broken his skull and his nose.

The door to the Duprees' home was still ajar, so they cautiously entered, not knowing whether the assailant was still inside. Nothing seemed to be disturbed; the rooms were neat and tidy. Going back into the supermarket, Inspector Van Vuuren bent down, and, running his hands down the side of Mr Dupree's trousers, felt a wallet in the trouser pocket, which he carefully drew out. Opening it, he found that it contained nearly $100 in cash, together with Mr Dupree's credit cards and driver's license. He handed these over to Constable Hardy, who by then had finished taking photos of Mrs Dupree. Inspector Van Vuuren and Sergeant Major Mpofu searched the store. None of the tills had been tampered with, and nothing appeared to have been stolen - except on the tool stand, where a shape in the dust suggested a missing hammer.

Inspector Van Vuuren reached the conclusion, and both Sergeant Major Mpofu and Constable Hardy agreed, that the killings had nothing to do with burglary. And there were no signs of a forced entry into the shop, which strongly suggested that whoever had committed this foul deed was someone known to the Duprees. Recalling James Johansson's information that there had been a party at the motel the previous night, the inspector decided to go over and speak to Mary Hartley. He put Sergeant Major Mpofu in charge of the scene and left Constable Hardy with him. They were to await the arrival of the coroner and search the shop for a discarded hammer.

'Inspector Van Vuuren, Mary is in her office. You can go straight in,' said Irene Van Der Merwe, the motel receptionist, as Ben entered the motel. Mary Hartley arose from her desk where she was.

'Oh, Inspector Van Vuuren ... this is truly horrible. We're all in a state of shock ... who could've done such a terrible thing? And to two of our most respected and loved people!' As she paused, Inspector Van Vuuren interjected:

'Well, that's why I'm here; wanted to know whether you had any people from out of town staying here last night.'

'Not that I can remember ... but let me have a look at the register, to make sure.' And with that Mrs Hartley buzzed reception. 'Bring the register in, please,' she asked. Within a few minutes the receptionist arrived and handed the register over to Mrs Hartley, who sat down and turned over the page to the night before. She looked through it slowly. Closing the register and turning to Inspector Van Vuuren she said:

'As I thought ... no, no one from out of town booked in last night ... in fact, no one from out of town even remaining here from the past few days.'

'How did the party go? Were you there?' asked Inspector Van Vuuren of Mary. On getting her affirmative reply, he asked, 'Did you see anything at all out of the ordinary during the party?' Mrs Hartley thought for a few moments, then said,

'No, no, not really. The only thing I can recall was that Jessica Dupree left early, as she had to drive through to Bulawadi. She was picking up Joseph Swanson today on his arrival from Zambanyika - at the airport ... Oh, my, she won't have heard. Oh, how terrible: poor Jessica ... ' and she trailed off into silence. After a few seconds she continued, 'Oh, yes, I remember seeing James Johansson leaving at one stage, but he came back later. Sorry, I didn't take note of the time.'

'Don't worry, Mary. I can find out details from them. Thanks for all your help - always appreciated,' and with that he left and walked back to the supermarket.

Returning to the supermarket, Inspector Van Vuuren was met by Sergeant Major Mpofu and Constable Hardy, who informed him that the coroner had been and that both bodies had been taken to the morgue. They had conducted a search but could not find anything resembling a hammer discarded anywhere within the premises, including the house. He thanked them both, and, as they left the building, Inspector Van Vuuren stopped suddenly and, bending down, picked up the remains of a cheroot lying on the step.

'Not saying that it's anything,' he mused, 'but, just in case, I'll have the DNA taken from it,' and with that he placed the cheroot into a plastic bag and sealed it. At this point, Inspector Van Vuuren heard Brian Moody, the local bank manager, call to him.

'Ben, can I have a word?' he asked. Inspector Van Vuuren looked up.

'Oh, hi, Brian. Yeah, of course,' he replied and walked up to Brian Moody who was standing outside the taped-off area.

'Of course, the whole town is shocked by this horrible murder of the Duprees.' Brian paused and continued: 'I was, as is usual, looking at the tape from the camera sited at the ATM outside the bank, and, well, although it's there to film those using the ATM, it's actually opposite the Duprees' store, and, well, looking at last night's tape, I could see, although it was very blurred, a white pick-up truck pull up outside the shop. Someone got out, went and knocked at the door and then it looks like Mrs Dupree opening the door and, after a brief conversation, inviting the person in … seems to indicate she knew the person.' Before he could continue, Inspector Van Vuuren interjected:

'Brian, can I have a look at this?' Brian Moody replied 'Well, of course, follow me over to the bank. I'll put it on again for you.'

Once inside Brian Moody's office, they sat down to watch the tape. It was just as Brian had described, although not clear enough to pick up a license plate, make of vehicle, or, for that matter, who the man was. But what it did show was that, some half-an-hour later. The man emerged from the building and returned to his truck before doing a strange thing: he took off his shirt and put on another one, before climbing back in and driving off.

'Now that's odd,' Inspector Van Vuuren remarked. 'Did you see that? He changed his shirt before driving off.'

'Yes, that's what got me thinking you should see this, too,' replied Brian. Inspector Van Vuuren thanked him and, taking the tape, left the bank and headed back to the store.

At the store, he sent Constable Hardy to the motel with orders that Constable White and he were to take James and Jenny Johansson back to the police station. He had some questions for them. Leaving two African constables at the front and two more at the back to stop anyone entering, he, together with Sergeant Major Mpofu, got into the police car and headed back to the police station.

On arrival they went straight into Inspector Ben Van Vuuren's office to wait for the two Johanssons. From the window, the inspector watched Constable Hardy arrive with James in James' truck. He was startled to note that it was a white Ford pick-up truck .

'Well, well,' he mused. 'Now is that a coincidence, or what?' He turned and went to his desk, where he sat down deep in thought. A few minutes later, he asked Sergeant Major Mpofu to fetch Jenny Johansson through for interview. Jenny was ushered to her seat and informed that the interview was being taped. Would she please relate what she could remember of the events from the previous evening's party at the motel? She described how she and her brother James had gone in his pick-up truck to the event and how she had a lovely time with all the other younger people that were there. When asked whether everyone had stayed till the end, she said,

'Yes, we all were having such a nice time.' Then she paused before continuing, 'Well, no, not all of us stayed. I remember now, Jessica Dupree left early, saying she had something or other to do. I can't really recall what. Jessica was addressing us all at the time and, with all the merriment, we just wished her Happy Christmas and she left.' Inspector Van Vuuren asked:

'No one else leave the party, then?'

'No, Jessica was the only one that I can remember.' Jenny frowned and closed her eyes for a while before continuing. 'Oh, wait, I remember my brother saying that he was going to top up his petrol tank, as he knew that the petrol station would be closed today. But he was only gone for about forty-five minutes before returning and joining us all again.' Inspector Van Vuuren thanked her and asked her to step out. Once she had been gone for a few minutes, he again sent out Sergeant Major Mpofu, to bring in her brother James this time. Nearly everyone in the town knew that Jessica had been going out not only with James Johansson but also with Joseph Swanson. Once seated, James was informed that the interview was being taped, and he too was asked about the previous evening's party. His account of the evening was pretty much as his sister's, except that, on being asked by Inspector Van Vuuren whether anyone had left early, he was quick to recall Jessica Dupree's departure, adding:

'Oh, and shortly after she left, I went and topped up my petrol, as I knew the petrol station would be closed today. After that I returned to the party and stayed till it finished. Then I took my sister home and went to bed before coming to town today. As you know, I wanted to wish the Duprees a Happy Christmas.' Then he related how he found the Duprees and had asked his sister to call the police, saying,

'What a horrible thing. Who in their right mind could do such a thing? Hope you catch the bastard responsible.' He paused, then said: 'Do you mind if I smoke?'

'No, not at all, go ahead,' replied the inspector. 'You know they're bad for you,' he laughed. And James laughed, too, saying,

'Yeah, I know, but what the heck!' He took out a cheroot from its packet and lit it, Inspector Van Vuuren noticing immediately that the cheroot was identical to the stub he had found at the scene. The inspector continued to talk with James another five to ten minutes, long enough for James to finish smoking his cheroot and stub it out in the ashtray. Inspector Van Vuuren thanked him for coming in and asked him whether he would be so kind as to send his sister back in again.

Jenny was asked once again to take a seat.

'Sorry, Jenny,' started Van Vurren, 'there's just something I was told but forgot to ask you and your brother.' He paused, cleared his throat and then asked, 'Last night, did you happen to notice that when your brother returned from the petrol station, he had a different shirt on?'

'Oh, heck!' replied Jenny, looking surprised. 'Yes, how did I forget? He said that, in his haste, he had spilled some petrol on his shirt front but luckily had a spare in his cab, so he changed and put it on. He didn't want to have that petrol smell on him.' She laughed, then said, 'Sorry.'

'No problem, it's just that observant Mrs Hartley had mentioned it,' lied the inspector, 'and I just wanted it confirmed, that's all. You may go, but please do send James back in, will you?'

'Sure,' responded Jenny, and she walked out. A few moments later, James was seated before Inspector Van Vuuren once again.

'Sorry, James, something I forgot to ask: it was noticed that when you came back in from filling up with petrol, you had a different shirt on. Any reason why?' James replied straight away:

'Yes, yes, I did. Yeah, I spilled some petrol down the front of my shirt ... nothing worse than that strong smell of petrol, but, lucky for me, I had a spare shirt in the cab, so changed before returning,' he said.

'No problem. Thanks, just wanted the change to be explained. Yeah, I agree, the smell of petrol is very strong. I can understand why you changed. Think I would have done the same.' He laughed, then suggested that James take his sister home. As the Johanssons left, Inspector Van Vuuren returned to his office, picked up the cheroot butt, put it in a package and sent it off to the forensic department in Bulawadi.

Two days later, and the town still in shock and horror at the brutal killings, Inspector Van Vuuren was sitting at his desk in his office at the police station when the phone rang. He picked it up, and the voice on the other end asked,

'Ben, is that you? It's David Taylor - Forensic Department - '

'Oh, hi, David,' cut in the Inspector. 'Belated Happy Christmas to you. What can I do for you?'

'Ah, Ben, more what I can do for you! Those cheroot stubs you sent me - DNA is same on both ... James Johansson. And there's more!' He paused.

'Come on, David, don't leave me hanging. What else do you have for me?'

'Well, seems young James Johansson has a history of being an angry young man when his girl friends dump him.' He paused, then continued. 'Whilst at college, when his then girl friend broke up with him, he keyed her car. Made a good job of it too. He was convicted and fined. But then, whilst working in Bulawadi, he got dumped again by his new girl friend. He retaliated by throwing a brick through her window. Again he was convicted and fined. So, I wonder, has young James been up to his tricks again?' David asked.

'Well, I don't know whether he'd been dumped or not. But those stubs - one was found at the scene of a murder. The other he smoked here at the station whilst being interviewed.'

'Oh, heck!' exclaimed David. 'Don't say he's moved on to murdering those who dump him, now!'

'Well, we don't know whether that was the case,' replied the inspector, 'but glad of the information, David. Cheers, matey!' He hung up.

Of course, a day ago, Jessica had returned from Bulawadi with Joseph Swanson to be met by Inspector Van Vuuren and informed of the horrible murders that had occurred. The inspector offered his sympathy, condolences and assurance that the police would do all they could to bring the person responsible to court. Joseph then drove a very distressed Jessica to his parents' farm, the Bar 8, where Betty Swanson looked after her. Inspector Van Vuuren had left her there to grieve, but now, armed with this latest information, he drove out to the Bar 8 to have a chat with Jessica.

Arriving at the homestead, he was met by Joseph, who, on being asked, stated that Jessica was holding up well, considering the circumstances, and said how shocked both he and his parents were at the murders. He ushered Inspector Van Vuuren into the lounge, where his father Bill sat smoking his pipe whilst Betty sat on the couch with her arm around Jessica's shoulders. Inspector Van Vuuren greeted them all and to Jessica re-stated his deepest sympathy and condolences.

'Jessica, if you feel up to it, I just want to ask you a question,' he said. Jessica raised her face and, looking at him, tears still running down her cheeks, said,

'Of course, Inspector. What would you like to know?'

'Well, it's about James Johansson. It's well known that you were going out with both Joseph and James, but on Christmas Eve, at the party, did you happen by any chance to tell James that he was no more in the picture?' Jessica looked at him, startled.

'Inspector Van Vuuren, how on earth would you have known that?' She paused, then continued, 'Well, yes, yes, I did, shortly before leaving the party and saying good-bye to all. Gosh, I know he was angry, but surely you don't think he attacked my mum and dad? No, not James!' The colour drained from her face, and she turned her head into Mrs Swanson's shoulder and sobbed uncontrollably.

Inspector Van Vuuren waited patiently until Jessica managed to regain some control and, when she turned to him, replied,

'Well, we can't say at this stage that it was James, but the young man does have a past record of retaliating against those who've dumped him - though in the past it's always been damaging their property, never harming them.' He looked over at her and continued: 'But our investigations are proceeding apace, and we do hope that very soon we'll be able to find out who was responsible. And we *will* bring whoever it was to justice, I promise you.' Then, thanking them all, he left and went back to the police station, calling in at the magistrates' for a warrant to search James Johansson's vehicle.

Once back at the police station, he sat at his desk and opened the file, going back over all the statements and lines of enquiry, carefully re-creating in his mind what had gone on that fateful Christmas evening.

'Blast!' he mused, once again. 'Murders don't even stop for Christmas!' Calling for Constable Hardy, he proceeded to the police car and headed out towards the Lazy J farm where, he told Constable Hardy, he had some questions for young James Johansson. Inwardly he was praying that James had not yet taken his shirt out of the cab, as he desperately wanted to have a look at that! They arrived at the Lazy J homestead and approached the front door, but, before Inspector Van Vuuren could knock, the door was opened by Patrick Johansson, who had observed their arrival.

'Hello, Inspector Van Vuuren. I'd wish you a Happy Christmas, but, with the horrible murders, it doesn't seem appropriate, really. Anyway, what can I do for you?' Inspector Van Vuuren asked whether James were in and, on receiving an affirmative from Patrick Johansson, asked whether he could speak with him.

'James, Inspector Van Vuuren here to see you,' called Patrick, and a few moments later James arrived. James greeted Inspector Van Vuuren and Constable Hardy and asked how he could help them. Inspector Van Vuuren, showing the search warrant, said, 'I'd like to look inside your pick-up truck.' James' heart sank, and for a brief moment he was shocked, wondering to himself why the inspector would want to do that. How would he know that he had put his blood-stained shirt in there? But then he smiled to himself, remembering that there was nothing in there. He had made sure of that!

'Of course, inspector, no problem,' and with that he led Van Vuuren and Hardy to the truck. Constable Hardy engaged James in general talk, whilst Inspector Van Vuuren opened the driver's door and slowly pulled the seat forward so he could look behind it. Not finding the shirt, he was a little disappointed, but, just as he was about to return the seat, something caught his eye. It was a small red smear on the bodywork. He drew out his bottle containing the cotton wool swab and, running it over the smear, it immediately indicated that it was human blood. He replaced it in the container, pushed the seat back and closed the door.

'Thanks, James, that's all I wanted to see.' With that, they all returned to the homestead where Inspector Van Vuuren said their goodbyes, and he and Constable Hardy returned to the station.

Arriving at the police station, Inspector Van Vuuren immediately phoned David Taylor at the Forensic Dept in Bulawadi.

'David, hi, I'm coming through with a blood-swab which I'd like you to test against the blood samples the hospital sent of both Mrs and Mr Dupree.' He paused, and David replied that he would be waiting. Inspector Van Vuuren thanked him, put down the phone, headed to the police car and drove off towards Bulawadi. He went directly to the forensic department, where he met David Taylor and handed over the sample. David did the necessary test and came back with a positive match for Mrs Dupree. Inspector Van Vuuren was elated, and, after getting the formal paperwork, proceeded back to Legion where he picked up Constable Hardy and headed back to the Lazy J homestead. A surprised Patrick Johansson answered their knocking on the door.

'Wasn't expecting you back, inspector. What can I do for you?' Inspector Van Vuuren asked to see James.

'James Johansson, I'm arresting you for the murder of Mr and Mrs Dupree.' James was cautioned and read his rights before being handcuffed and taken back to the station. James Johansson, protesting his innocence all the while, was taken to the charge office where the inspector confronted him with the evidence: of his truck observed on the bank's video, including his changing his shirt at the supermarket; then the cheroot at the scene; his cheroot-stub at the police station with his DNA on it; his previous antics following past break-ups; then finally the blood-swab taken from his truck and its matching Mrs Dupree's blood. At this point, James broke down and confessed all.

One month later, James Johansson was found guilty of the murder of both Mrs and Mr Dupree. James told how he had gone to the supermarket hoping to confront Jessica over her dumping him. He had thought Mrs Dupree was lying. Having let him in, and being asked of Jessica's whereabouts, she had said she was in Bulawadi. He told how, in his anger, he had reached over and grabbed the hammer and had struck her several times with it. Her screams had Mr Dupree coming from the home and of course, having now seen James, he also had to be killed to stop him telling all.

The jury found him guilty, and he got a total of sixty years for the double murder. The Town of Legion settled down to life once again, but not the normal life as it had been before this Christmas-time murder. This murder would be in the minds of all the inhabitants for years to come, and they would echo Inspector Van Vuuren's thoughts: 'Murders don't stop even at Christmas.'

Mummy, mummy, Santa's here!
Peter Hodgson

There was something in the air that night. A peculiar unease came over Jackie, an unwelcome feeling that was about to spoil a perfectly enjoyable evening amongst friends. Perhaps it was something to do with the film they had just watched. Jackie couldn't remember the title, but a particular scene began to surface in her mind as she walked into the kitchen. Jackie shook her head and reminded herself that it was just a film and, after all, it was supposed to be the happiest time of the year. Christmas was fast approaching. This year her husband, Nick, had bought a real Christmas tree to replace the fibre-optic one they'd purchased three years earlier. Their little daughter called it 'Santa's big tree where the pretty fairy lives on top.' Chloe was so excited knowing that Santa was coming to town with presents galore stuffed inside his big sack.

Jackie reached for the chilled bottle and poured three dry Chablis for herself and two friends, Andrea and Holly. She looked out of the window, saw nothing but the black night. Without thinking, she switched the radio on and listened to the smooth voice of Dean Martin. She sang the words of the song: *It doesn't show signs of stopping, and I've bought some corn for popping. The lights are turned way down low. Let it snow, let it snow, let it snow ...* It would be nice to have snow for a change, Jackie thought. She joined her friends in the cosy, dimly-lit living room and lowered the tray of drinks on to the coffee table. Jackie sat on the thick rug and bathed in the warm orange glow of the fire.

'Thanks, Jackie,' Andrea said, after taking a sip of the wine.

'I thought the film was boring, a bit typical,' Holly remarked.

'Quite creepy,' Andrea added. 'The swimming pool ... ' She hesitated as if something had interrupted her train of thought.

'Yes, go on,' Jackie prompted. 'What about the swimming pool?'

'Well, when the girl in the red dress fell into the pool, you know, when the killer was chasing her in the dark, that's when I was reminded of my fear of pool lights. I'm frightened of swimming pools that have lights on the interior walls. During the day it doesn't bother me. At night, when a pool is lit up, I can't stand to go anywhere near it. I can't explain why it affects me that way.'

'Irrational fears,' Holly said, her voice coarse and low to give a creepy effect. 'So, when did you become aware of this?'

'Craig and I went on holiday to Portugal about ten years ago. At night all the pools near to the apartments were lit up. The water was smooth, still and unsettling. Perhaps I fell into a pool when I was a child, or saw some horrid creature with glowing eyes surfacing from a cold murky lake whilst having a bad dream. Who knows?'

'I hate spiders,' Holly said. 'Not the little ones. Every now and then a big black spider comes into our house. I suppose it's the cold driving them in.'

'And what do you do when you see one?' Jackie asked.

'Nothing. I just freeze and shout for Adam to come and squash it. Sometimes he's not quick enough, and it runs away to hide somewhere. It's the anticipation of it running away that gives me the shivers. They're so incredibly fast for a small creature. I hate them.'

'Arachnophobia,' Andrea said, the flash of her expensive gold necklace skimming across Jackie's eyes. 'That's fear of spiders, isn't it?'

'You're correct,' Holly said, wanting to change the subject. 'And before you ask, I *have* seen the film starring Jeff Daniels.'

'An old film,' Andrea said. Jackie finished her drink. Her lips tightened. Her turn next. She could opt out and say that nothing frightened her, but Holly would know she wasn't telling the truth. She knew more about her friend's past than anyone else. She knew how vulnerable she had become since those dreadful events of the previous year. Jackie looked up at them and said,

'Santaphobia.'

'Santaphobia,' Andrea repeated. 'I've never heard of it.'

'I didn't think I'd ever get round to telling anyone about it. I don't like Santa Claus. Never have.' Andrea giggled. Holly pressed her finger against her lips, signalling Andrea to be quiet.

'All those years ago, and I can still remember the occasion,' Jackie continued. 'We lived in Cheltenham in those days. Mum and dad took me into town and bought me a lovely doll. We looked round for a while, and I saw him. He was sitting next to a big Christmas tree surrounded by sacks full of toys.'

'Just a normal Santa,' Andrea said.

'Yes. He looked like all the others, I suppose. This particular one was wearing white gloves, and his fingers were wriggling all the time. He kept staring at me whilst I waited for my turn. He wore these little round glasses and had malevolent eyes. I got this feeling that he wanted to possess me, to have me all for himself.'

'Did you sit on his knee, then?' Andrea asked, a flippant tone in her voice.

'Yes. When it came to my turn, I was petrified. His breath was foul, and his long white beard kept tickling my face. He had a high-pitched voice, sort of compressed; and his cheeks were red and bulging. I remember screaming and reaching out for my dad.'

'The experience has turned you against Santa,' Holly said. Jackie nodded.

'It's a fear that I can't explain. That very same night, I had a nightmare. Santa is squeezing me tightly and I can't breathe. I'm trying to cry for help … ' Jackie fell silent, as if reliving her dream. ' … but my voice won't come out, no matter how hard I try. Mum and dad are laughing insanely whilst Santa's words come out faster and faster. Suddenly he stops talking and then … ' Andrea was standing by the window, peering into the back garden.

'And then?' she said.

' … he speaks again, and his voice sounds like that of a wicked old woman.' Jackie was beginning to feel nervous. The creepy film they had watched, coupled with all this talk about phobias, had created a certain disquiet. She joined her friend at the window and asked what the matter was. Holly came by her side and gently squeezed her hand. Jackie smiled. There was something about

Holly that radiated rationality and calm. And now the three women were standing together by the window. The garden at the rear of the detached house had a wooden fence and bushes as its boundary. Beyond the fence there was nothing except fields and a few patches of trees.

'I thought I heard a noise,' Andrea said. Jackie put her hand to her mouth and felt a slight acceleration of her heart.

'I'm sure I saw a light flicker,' Holly murmured. 'Look: there it is!' Beyond the garden they saw a pale glow that seemed to rise and fall. Then, unexpectedly, the sound of a branch snapping. Jackie displayed no outward reaction. Youngsters often played in the fields, but not at this time of the night. Whatever it was, the light went out.

Jackie went upstairs. Chloe was safe and fast asleep. She tucked her in, ran her hand gently across her forehead, admiring her rosy cheeks and blonde curls resting on the pillow. The laughter coming from downstairs annoyed her. Nothing funny had occurred during the evening. Why are they laughing? she thought, and wished she hadn't told them about her fear of Father Christmas and the horrible dream so firmly embedded in her memory. Their phobias had been brushed aside and dismissed. Andrea's phobia was something that could be easily avoided, and Holly's fear of spiders seemed trivial enough. As Jackie turned to go downstairs, she realised that Chloe was now old enough to go shopping with her, and maybe she would ask to see Santa in town. He would sit her on his knee and ask what she wanted for Christmas.

When Jackie entered the living room, she heard car doors slamming shut, and the sound of laughter. Their husbands had returned. Nick turned the key and pushed the door open.

'What's the matter? You all right?' he said to Jackie. She said yes. Adam followed Nick into the living room. Craig closed the door.

'It's snowing,' he said and kissed her on the cheek. She could smell alcohol mixed with an expensive but ostentatious aftershave.

He was dressed expensively: Ralph Lauren chino trousers, zip suede jacket, Langbury leather brogues. He liked to show off his wealth in any way he could. He joined the others. Andrea wasn't pleased to see him. He bent down, planted a kiss on Holly's forehead and said how lovely she looked. Jackie was nauseated by his superficial charm. He fell into a comfy armchair and motioned Andrea to sit on the arm. Nick asked Jackie whether she wouldn't mind making some tea, then went upstairs to check on Chloe.

'So, which pub did you go to?' Holly asked.

'Same place as usual,' Adam replied.

'The Scraggy Hen,' Andrea said wearily, giving Craig a sardonic smile.

'A beautiful, atmospheric pub,' he added. His alcoholic breath was already beginning to annoy his wife. 'You don't care much for the Scraggy Hen, do you?'

'I don't like some of the people who go there,' Andrea replied. 'We all know why you like it so much, Craig. It attracts loose, chatty women. It's more like a knocking shop nowadays, so I've heard.' Adam laughed. Holly squeezed his arm, not wanting him to trivialise Andrea's disapproval of the popular drinking venue. Jackie had been listening to the conversation. She poured hot water into the cups and peered out of the window, fearful of what she might see. There was no moving light. She turned around just as Craig walked in, his shifty eyes running down her body.

'Enjoyable evening for you?' she asked, adding milk to the teas.

'You could say that. I believe you lot watched a thriller. Was it any good?'

'Oh, it was okay,' she answered, reaching to the floor for a spoon that had fallen from her hand and bounced under the table. He took a few steps forward, and the small change of position, apparently so trivial, confirmed the notion that he was looking down the top of her blouse. When she straightened herself, he was staring at her, waiting for some kind of response. 'Help me with these teas,' she said.

'Right you are, milady.' For the next half hour, Jackie and Nick Stevens entertained their guests as best they could. Nick played a CD of popular Christmas songs, and they all talked about what they were doing over the festive period. By the time their friends were ready to leave, Jackie was even more subdued and dreading the thought of a departing kiss from Craig. She couldn't escape that.

When Jackie woke up the following morning, the light shining in from outside seemed strangely intense. She pulled open the curtains and saw white roof tops and tree branches covered with fluffy snow. She dressed and went downstairs. Nick had just finished his breakfast and was ready for work.

"Morning, sweetheart,' he said. 'I must be off. I've had a call from the other side of town. Burst water pipe. And there are four other jobs for me to do.'

'Has Chloe had breakfast?'

'I gave her some Coco Pops,' Nick replied, taking his coat off the wall hook. 'Be careful. It's thick with snow out there.'

'I will. See you later.' Nick kissed her and went to work. Chloe was watching *The Snowman*, all nice and warm in her pink penguin onesie. Mum smiled at her and wished she and her friends had watched an enjoyable family film instead of an eerie thriller. The film was still playing on her mind.

A minute later, she was in the kitchen. She switched the kettle on, inserted bread into the toaster. She opened the back door and looked beyond the garden at the smooth snow-carpeted fields, undisturbed by human activity. She then opened the cupboard door and paused. The tablets she was so used to taking were not there anymore. She quickly pulled her hand away, told herself that she wouldn't be needing those again. And her mind wandered to the day when her life had been turned upside-down, when everyone she knew seemed suspicious of her - a period that was so vague and terrible. The kettle clicked off. Bread popped out of the toaster. Jackie picked up butter and knife, when a noise caught her attention. She could hear a faint rhythmic jingle coming from outside. She stood at the open back door, looking for any movement amidst the white blaze of snow-covered fields. When she looked to her left she saw him. He was twenty yards away, and looking in her direction - a black figure against a white background. What is he doing round here? What does he want? she thought. And when her eyes drifted to the garden, she saw what he had left behind.

PC Adam Wilkins arrived at home in the evening, two hours later than usual. Holly was used to his late hours.

'Been busy today?' she asked, after they had settled in front of a hot gas-fire. She was sipping tea and cradling the saucer on her lap.

'We usually are busy. Everywhere is busy at this time of the year; even in Evesham. I had to chase a shoplifter today. It made me realise how unfit I am.'

'You're not unfit, Adam. Not really. Was it a man who you chased?'

'A young man. I caught up with him at the Pizza Pomodoro. I was almost tempted to go in and order a bite to eat. What have you been up to?'

'Cleaning this place and playing with Macy's new pet.'

'Not another dog, is it?'

'Yep. He's a puppy, and they're calling him "Samson".'

'Great name,' Adam said.

'Oh, and Jackie rang this afternoon. She's not a happy woman.'

'I thought she was a bit withdrawn the other night. You should have watched a pleasant film, not something that would make her feel nervous.'

'It wasn't my idea. Andrea suggested we watch it … Jackie saw a young man at the back of her house this morning. She thought he was watching her. She was frightened, and Nick had already gone to work.'

'I see. She had a bad time during her last job, didn't she? All that trouble because of one man. But she's got over that now. It's all in the past.' Adam took a sip of Baileys Irish Cream, looked into Holly's beautiful brown eyes and rested his arm on her shoulder. Holly fell into silence, her thoughts concentrating on her friend. She knew that Nick would always be there for Jackie, no matter what.

The following morning, Jackie didn't let on to Nick that she'd had a poor night's sleep. There would be nothing he could do about it, anyway. The bad dream she'd had was clear in her memory ... *The shopping mall is brightly lit with thousands of bulbs. The floor is alive with black hairy spiders. The indoor fountain is pumping coloured water. Red water. Or is it blood? He is there, sitting on a big chair made of holly. Father Christmas is ringing his bell and singing the same nonsensical line over and over. Father Christmas dressed in black, rocking to and fro. She is floating towards him. He desperately wants to touch her. Then she will die. She can smell his sour odour as she moves closer to him. His thin fingers are wriggling, his arm stretching longer and longer ... until the final touch.* And Jackie woke up. Nick came downstairs in his dressing-gown. A well-cooked breakfast was waiting for him.

'You look tired, sweetheart,' he said, taking a seat at the table.

'I went to bed early,' she said, a hint of annoyance in her voice. 'I didn't sleep so well, though.'

'I'm sorry I was late. I took another call on the way home. You know how it is. Are you feeling all right?' She shook her head and told him about the man she had seen. Nick decided to have a look in the back garden. The bright sun was reflecting off the hardened snow.

'Where was he when you saw him?'

'Over in that direction,' she said. 'He was staring at me ... Oh, Nick, what are we going to do? He could be stalking me.'

'Now let's not be silly, Jackie. Someone was taking a walk. You've been through enough already.'

'Look at those footprints then - his footprints.' Nick took a closer look at the prints. The impressions made by the left foot were turned inwards, indicating some kind of deformity.

'There's nothing to be scared of. Michael has been here.'

'Michael?'

'He lives a few houses down the road. He has this peculiar walk. His left foot is angled inwards, you see.'

'Well, I've never seen him before.'

'Jackie, we haven't been in this house that long. Michael lives with his parents. He has learning difficulties, or something like that. I only know because they once called me into their house to fix a leaky tap.' A young man dressed in black. Watching. Stalking. A neighbour with a psychological impairment. Jackie didn't like it.

'And look,' Nick said, pointing at a particular spot on the ground. Jackie could see the small animal tracks. 'Those are his cat's prints,' he explained. 'He came into our garden because he was looking for his beloved cat.' Nick embraced her. 'Happy now?' he said. Jackie swept her long auburn hair off her face and forced a smile.

'I love you, Nick. I'll be fine.'

'Good. What are your plans for today?'

'I need to do some shopping, really. I haven't been out for months. I must do something to get my confidence back.'

'Shall we go together?'

'No. You stay here and look after Chloe. I'll drive into town.'

'Well, if you're sure about this.'

'I can do it, Nick. Really, I can.'

'Be careful, then. The roads will be treacherous.' The phone rang and Nick answered. Jackie got into her coat and wrapped a thick scarf round her neck. Chloe ran to her side.

'Mummy, can I come shopping with you?' she asked.

'Some other time, sweetheart,' Jackie said, frowning.

'Oh, please. I want to see Santa. Please, mummy.' Nick joined them.

'We could take Chloe into town tomorrow,' he said. 'That would be exciting for her. If a job comes in, I'll just have to delay it.' Jackie's frown deepened.

'We'll see. Who was that on the phone?'

'Wrong number.' Wrong number again, she thought. That's the second time this week. Who's trying to upset me?

Going shopping on her own was something that she had to do. Nick would have gone with her, no problem; but she had to make the effort. Chloe was tugging her coat. The look on her face was saying, *Please.* Jackie promised to take her into town the next day. She kissed Nick and went on her way. Chloe was at the window, her little hand waving goodbye. The drive to the supermarket was slow and tedious. She couldn't ignore the images that were surfacing in her mind: Michael standing silent and motionless, his figure black against the dazzling white snow; the eerie light moving about in the dark; footprints leading up to the house; Father Christmas dressed in black. Twenty minutes later she was amongst shoppers pushing trolleys. Chris Rea's 'Driving Home for Christmas' was playing in the background. Jackie liked that song. Today, nothing could make her heart lighter. She picked a chocolate Santa off the shelf and cringed.

'That can go back where it came from,' she said. She studied her list of items: turkey, mince-pies, cranberry sauce, crackers, tinsel, cards and so on. The task ahead temporarily eased her troubled mind.

Jackie felt a sense of accomplishment when she reached the car. She loaded her bags in the boot and pushed the trolley back to the bay. The boot was left open. When she returned, she noticed an envelope on top of a carrier bag. She ripped it open and took out a Christmas card showing a smiling Santa about to climb down a chimney. She read the one line that had been handwritten: *You could make my dreams come true.* A car's horn beeped. Her eyes followed the green car as it took the bend leading away from the parking area. The driver was wearing a fur-trimmed Santa Claus hat. She was almost certain that Craig was the driver. She would tell Nick all about the torment she was experiencing. He would comfort her as he had done in the past.

Jackie drove home at a crawling speed. As she turned into Oliver Road, she saw a man standing near her house. She experienced a flutter of panic. As she got closer, he turned to look at her. His face carried a haunted, sad expression. She stopped the car in order to speak to him. Michael looked to the ground and walked off. She shouted his name. He ignored her, walking away in that distinctive manner: his left foot pointing inwards.

Inside the house she found a note from Nick saying he had gone to see a friend. Chloe was with him. Jackie put the shopping away whilst ruminating over Craig's stupid little game and Michael's unwelcome presence at the driveway. She looked out of the window, but there was no sign of him. Then she remembered the card that Craig and Andrea had sent to their home. She checked to see whether the handwriting matched the card left for her at the supermarket. They didn't match. She threw them on to the floor just as the phone started ringing. She answered. No reply.

'Who is this? … What do you want?' She listened for a few seconds and ended the call. A noise from outside sent her dashing into the back garden. 'Shoo!' she shouted. 'Go away!' A hungry cat scurried off. Jackie cringed at the sound of the little bell attached to its collar. She closed her eyes tightly and swore under her breath. 'That's it,' she said. 'Enough is enough.'

She got in the car and headed for Broadway Road, to the home of Craig and Andrea McKenna. When she arrived at the house, she saw a movement in the bedroom window and wondered whether he was expecting to see her. She walked up the pathway and stopped for a brief look at his metallic-green Mercedes. She rang the doorbell. Andrea answered.

'Where is Craig?' Jackie asked.

'He's in there,' she replied, sensing trouble. The living room was warm and spacious. The colour of the bespoke carpet matched the plush grey sofa and chairs. A blue coral chandelier hung from the ceiling. There were no trimmings, only a three-foot fibre-optic tree standing in a corner and looking somewhat insignificant. Craig was relaxing in a chair, looking smarmy in his Armani dressing gown.

'What's all this about?' she said, handing him the card. She was not prepared for the expression of shock that leaped upon his face.

'I don't know what you're talking about.'

'You're trying to scare me, aren't you? And what about the silent phone calls, eh?'

'This is ridiculous. Why should I want to scare you?' Andrea motioned her to sit down. She shook her head and marched out of the house. Andrea studied the card for a moment.

'It's definitely not your handwriting,' she said. 'We haven't known Jackie and Nick Stevens for that long, and now this happens … Well?'

'I'm sure I don't know what you mean.'

'Don't deceive me, Craig. I know about your flirtatious ways, and the affair you had with Stella Price. I'm warning you, Craig, don't you dare upset any of my friends. Not now. Not ever.'

Jackie was in the car, striking the steering wheel out of frustration. She phoned Nick, only to hear that they would be home later in the day. She felt better having heard his voice. She loved him so much and wished they could spend more time together. Driving home was difficult. Snow falling again, hindering her concentration. Her head was filled with murmuring voices. Pedestrians were a blur of constantly moving black shapes.

'See here, now,' Jackie said. 'I'm braver than you are. Nobody can make me fall apart. Nick is mine. Forever. So drown in your sea of despair.'

Holly knew something was wrong. Jackie had called to see them and was sitting opposite Adam. She was fidgety and stumbling over her words.

'Slow down,' Adam said to her, 'and take your time.'

'I'm sorry,' she said, looking up to the ceiling. Holly gave her a glass of port wine. She slowly drank it all and told them what had happened at the supermarket. Holly asked whether she thought Craig had put the card on top of her shopping.

'It was him alright. I saw him driving off. He's crazy.'

'What did Andrea have to say?'

'I don't know. I left in a hurry.' Jackie's expression was one of foreboding. 'And we've had phone calls, too,' she went on. 'It's the wrong number if Nick answers. If I answer, the caller says nothing. Craig McKenna is doing it to me.' Holly believed what she was telling them. Adam was unconcerned.

'And Michael was waiting for me when I returned home. He prowls about at night, shining a torch.'

'Who is he?' Holly asked.

'He lives a few doors down from their house,' Adam said. 'Most of us at the station have heard of Michael Niles. A strange one, he is. Wanders about town on his own. He's harmless enough. And it's not unusual for people to ring the wrong number - '

'But Craig is the guilty one. He's following me!'

'I believe Craig is a womaniser and plays jokes on people,' Holly said.

'It's not funny. Does he think for one minute I could ever love him?' Jackie got up and fell into her friend's open arms. Holly assured her there was nothing to worry about.

'Don't be like this,' she said softly. 'It will soon be Christmas Day. Think of all those lovely presents you've bought for Nick and Chloe.' She showed her to the door and kissed her cheek. 'Ring if you need me, Jackie.'

Holly closed the door. Jackie could feel her shoes crunching on the snow, and, as she passed Adam's car, something caught her eye. She looked in the back of the car and saw a Santa Claus outfit lying on the seat. Dean Martin's 'Let it Snow' was echoing in her head, and, when she turned to look at the house, her eyes drifted to the bedroom window. Somebody was watching her - a face peering from a gap in the curtains. A pale face. Small black eyes. Dead eyes. Thin lips mouthing silent words: I want you. I want you. I want you … Jackie shut her eyes tightly and felt the energy draining from her body. And when she opened them she saw a tiny hand waving to her.

Christmas Eve. Nick had decided to take them into town. He was driving the car and concentrating on the icy roads. Jackie was quiet. He was used to that, accustomed to her dark moods. Hopefully she would be back to normality the next day. He couldn't wait to see Chloe opening her presents, and how would Jackie react to the elegant gold drop-earrings she'd always wanted? Ten minutes later, they arrived at the shopping mall. Chloe's sparkling eyes were searching for Santa. The mall was dominated by a thirty-foot tree surrounded by huge flickering candles. Chloe was mesmerised by the countless pale blue lights and imitation silver snowflakes. Jackie put on a brave face and tried to assure herself that nothing would spoil the day. Nick moved on a few paces, keeping his eye on Chloe. They followed her through a crowd, and Jackie saw him sat on a plush red chair next to a plump Christmas tree, fairy lights blinking slowly, tinsel dancing in the waft of a nearby fan. A shiver rippled through her body. She could not look at the foul spectacle for more than a few seconds. She could not bear to see Chloe upon his knee.

'Look, Jackie. Chloe's waving to you,' Nick said.

'Oh, yes … It's a long queue, Nick. You stay here with Chloe. I'll have a look in that shop. I might find an extra gift for her.' Jackie made her way to the shop. She heard someone call out her name. The general chatter suddenly stopped, and everyone seemed to be staring at her. She looked at Santa again. Felt compelled to. He was beckoning her to release Chloe into his care. Those dreadful eyes, she thought. He wants Chloe. He wants to possess her everlasting soul. My pretty daughter. My eternal love. His bearded face moved closer to hers. Their daughter's arms are outstretched. She needs mummy to save her. Jackie is unable move a muscle or utter a single word. She screamed inside her head.

'Is there anything I can help you with?' the pretty shop assistant asked. Jackie was looking through the shop window at the parents with their children. She turned to the assistant, who asked whether something was the matter.

'I'm sorry. My mind was wandering,' Jackie said. 'I thought … ' She paused and looked towards the crowd again.

'Would you like something for your daughter? I saw you with her a moment ago.'

'Did you? Well, yes, I would like to buy something for her. Thank you.' The girl left her for a while and returned with a little musical reindeer. She pressed his red nose, and he started singing: *Rudolph the red-nosed reindeer, had a very shiny nose, and if you ever saw him, you would even say it glows.*

'That will do nicely,' Jackie said.

She waited outside the shop and saw Chloe running towards her, carrying a colouring book and a box of crayons.

'Look what Santa gave me, mummy!' She said.

Jackie made a weak smile and felt relieved that Chloe's meeting with Santa was over and done with.

In the early evening, the falling snow had created a smooth white blanket over the fields. Jackie looked out of the window, her eyes searching in vain for any movement or strange lights. She began preparing the vegetables for the following day. She would try her best to make this year's festive season a happy one. Nick was wrapping presents in the bedroom, out of Chloe's sight. Chloe was watching *The Grinch*, a wonderful film that would keep her occupied whilst mummy and daddy tended to other matters.

By 8.30 Chloe was tucked away in bed and feeling so excited that she was bound to be awake for at least another hour. Jackie poured herself a drink. The phone rang. Oh, no. Who can it be? she wondered. She was happy to hear Holly's voice and told her she was feeling fine. Holly was pleased. She said she had also been to the mall that day, with Adam by her side carrying the heavy bags. Holly said she would keep in touch.

Jackie was looking forward to an evening with her beloved Nick. There were lots of great films to choose from. She decided to have a bath first, then wash her hair. The phone rang again as Nick was coming downstairs. Jackie took the call and gave the handset to him.

'It's for you,' she said. Nick's expression told her that something was amiss. 'I see,' he said. 'Have you tried Josh's number? … Okay, I'll be there soon as I can.'

'What's the matter?' Jackie asked.

'The Crescent Hotel have a problem - '

'You can't go now, Nick.'

'It shouldn't take long. Don't start worrying. Have a couple of drinks. Relax.'

'Oh, all right. I would have thought the Crescent Hotel could cope with any emergency, even at this time of the year.'

Nick went on his way. Jackie watched a re-run of Christmas hit-records on TV. As time passed by, she could feel the anxiety flowing into her blood. She went upstairs and looked in on Chloe, who was pretending to be asleep. She ran a hot bath and looked out of the window to see whether Nick's van was in sight. He'll probably arrive home whilst I'm in the bath, she thought. I'll have some more wine later. Plenty of it. Twenty minutes later, she was dressed in her soft warm gown, running a brush through her wet hair and admiring her reflection in the mirror. Her eyes suddenly grew bigger.

A distant voice shattered the calm of the house. A ghostly voice from the past, as if emanating from some half-forgotten experience in her life. She mouthed her name in unison with the person who was repeating her name. This is no dream, she thought. This is really happening. Silence once again. She crept into the spare bedroom and made a gap in the curtains. She saw the light, the same pale glow she had seen when in the company of her two friends. Her heart was throbbing within her chest. She ran back into her own room and called Nick on her mobile. The ring tone seemed to last for ages. Eventually he answered.

'Thank goodness you're there,' she said. 'Is this job going to take forever?' Nick was oblivious to the panic in her voice. He promised he would be home in thirty minutes. He ended the call. Jackie went to see whether the strange light was still there. Nothing. She looked into the garden and could make out a recent set of footprints leading to the house. She ran downstairs, her mind swirling with trepidation. Everything was locked and safe. She listened to an ominous silence. Seconds later she was sitting in front of the mirror again, drying her long hair and wondering whether she should call the police. She decided to wait for Nick. She spent several minutes sitting there in her angst, and Chloe's reflection suddenly appeared in the mirror. She pressed her little hands together and cried,

'Mummy, mummy, Santa's here!'

'What are you talking about, Chloe?'

'He's here. Come and see.' Santa was slowly climbing the stairs, the sound of his heavy footsteps echoing throughout the house. A big green sack hung from his shoulder. She looked on him in horror. His red cheeks were like ripe apples. His smile was hidden beneath his long white beard. He spoke to them, his voice compressed and menacing, not human:

'Merry Christmas, Chloe. Merry Christmas to everybody.' Chloe ran back to her room and got into bed. Little children were not supposed to see Santa, otherwise he would not leave any presents for them. Jackie shrunk back from the hideous figure standing in front of her. Without thinking she ran into the bedroom and grabbed one of Nick's golf clubs that he'd left in a corner next to the wardrobe. Crazy with fear and panic she swung the club for all she was worth. A ribbon of skin flew through the air. Santa's head opened up, blood streaming into his evil eyes. He staggered backwards, hands clawing at the air as he fought to maintain his balance. Jackie screamed as his body flipped over the sharp turn of the staircase, its steel balusters standing firm. She heard the sickening sound of breaking bones as his head smashed into the floor. Chloe came out of her room, crying and shaking with distress. Jackie told her to go back inside and stay there. She grabbed her mobile, pressed the buttons on the keypad until she came to Adam's number. She blurted out her words and repeated them until Adam could understand what she was saying.

The door bell rang a short while later. Jackie could barely move one foot in front of the other as she descended the stairs. The intruder was moaning and trying to pull the beard away from his contorted face. She could hear the intake of his breath, struggling against the blood gurgling in his throat. She ran to the front door and pulled it open.

'Over there!' she cried. 'In the passage leading to the kitchen.' Adam went to have a look. He knelt beside the broken body, removed the hat and false beard, checked for a pulse. Holly closed the door behind her and froze. She looked around the place and gasped when she saw a red pool on the floor, close to the bottom of the staircase and growing in size. Her friend stood in front of her, shattered and totally confused.

'Footprints!' she screamed. 'They're his footprints. Somehow he got in by forcing the back door. I saw a light over the fields, and *his* footprints. He's coming for Chloe. He wants her all to himself. I know for sure … ' And now her body was shaking. Adam drew back the curtains and looked out of the window. He turned to face them.

'Jackie. Listen to me, Jackie. There are no footprints in the garden.' She took a few steps towards him.

'You're lying, Adam. I saw them. He came here to take Chloe. He's mad. Mad I tell you.' Adam shook his head.

'No, Jackie. You're wrong,' he said, his voice cracking with emotion. 'Your husband is dead. You've murdered Nick. He's dead.'

'No. It can't be him. It's not him. He loves me. Loves Chloe. He would never wear anything like that to frighten me. Never!'

'Didn't Nick tell you? I kept the outfit for him, Jackie. He wanted to surprise Chloe.'

'You never mentioned any of this to me. I can't believe this has happened,' Holly said, struggling to make sense of it all. 'Why didn't you tell me, Adam? How could you keep me from knowing?'

'Knowing what? I don't understand.' Adam punched a number into his phone and called for assistance. He picked up the sack of presents, and a familiar tune sounded from within it: *All of the other reindeers, used to laugh and call him names; they never let poor Rudolph, join in any reindeer games …*

Jackie fell to her knees. Santa was laughing insanely inside her head. When she looked towards the stairs, she saw crimson blood snaking towards her - the essence of *his* evil.

And if it touches her, she will die.

Partridge in the Pear Tree
Neal James

1

The week before Christmas and my luck is definitely out. I had hoped to be at home with my wife and daughter on Christmas Eve, but that idea was doomed to failure as soon as the shift-rotas were distributed. I'm Andy Mellors, DI at 'C' Division of the Derbyshire Constabulary at Ripley. There's only three days to go until the big day, and I'm fed up. Molly, our little girl, was expecting daddy to be at home on Christmas Eve to get ready for Santa's visit down the chimney – she'll face a lot of such disappointments as she grows up. As for me, I just have to get on with it; fifteen years in the force have got me this far, and it's not a career that I'd consider giving up lightly.

As I get out of my car, the snow, which began falling as I left our Oakwood home, has thickened, but it's turning to slush as soon as it hits the ground – perfect for wet feet! Grumpy? You bet I am, and now, just as I enter the station, the waving hand of Geoff Stokes, the desk sergeant, has me wandering over to see what he wants.

'Right up your street, this one, Andy.' He smiled – so he should, right at the end of *his* shift. He shouldn't be so familiar according to regulations, but we were at school together, so I let it slide. 'Nice tasty corpse for you out at Heanor.'

'Thanks a bunch, mate.' There was no lightness in my reply. I had hoped for a hot cuppa before setting out into the cold once again. 'Got the details?'

'Gave them to your DS.' He nodded to the stairs. 'Bit keener than you on days like this.'

Steve Parker had been my sergeant for almost a year, and Geoff was right – he was very keen. In fact he was a little too conscientious for my liking at times; I definitely needed to slow him down – he was making me look bad. I took the stairs two at a time to show a similar level of interest and breathed hard at the top of the third flight as I turned into the corridor leading to our offices and squad room. Parker smiled as I came through the door.

"Morning, guv.' He waved the crime report as I took off my coat. 'Body found this morning on the Heanor Gate Industrial Estate.' I nodded and sat down.

'Stokes told me as soon as I got through the door. Details?'

'Sketchy at the moment. Male, mid-thirties, with what looks like a blow to the back of the head,' he replied. 'We've been called out urgently – pathologist's already on site.'

'Bostock?'

'Yep, and he's running the show at the moment. Won't let any of the uniforms near the place.' Harry Bostock had been area pathologist for over twenty-five years and was an intimidating figure for any young copper to face. I knew how to handle him, and Parker was learning fast, but the beat coppers were all in awe – they'd all been watching too much TV.

'Come on, then.' I grabbed my coat, but was second out of the door as my sergeant headed off down the corridor.

The address given to us was an industrial unit on Delves Road, one of the main routes through the industrial estate just outside Heanor and off the main Derby Road. The journey was a short one, and with Parker at the wheel it gave me time to marshal my thoughts. I read through the report, and my heart sank. The body had been found by the cleaner early that morning at around seven, when she began work. She was still on-site and in the company of a female PC pending our arrival. We'd question her after a quick look at the body. Hopefully, by that time Bostock would be a little more amenable; he was less tolerable than me at being called out to an early event. Twenty minutes after leaving HQ, we arrived at Pear Tree House, the offices of PM Micro Electronics. Harry Bostock was just leaving as we stepped out of the car. The look on his face told me much of what I needed to know. There would be little in the way of detail until he was back at the lab, but it was always worth a try.

''Morning, Harry.' I smiled – it was an effort. 'Any preliminaries?' He stopped, scowled and put his bag in his car before turning back to me.

'White male, mid-thirties. Dead between eight and ten hours, according to liver temperature. Blunt-force trauma to the back of the head probably killed him outright, but I'll know for certain later. Your boys are scouring the site, but there was no weapon at the scene. Can I go now?' The speech was delivered with all the skill of a practised actor on the stage at the Derby Playhouse, and he was in his car and away before I had the time to reply.

'Cheery soul, as always.' Parker smirked; it hadn't taken him long to weigh Bostock up. 'Shall we?' He waved an arm in the direction of the entrance to the building.

'Pear Tree?' I pointed at the sign above the main entrance.

'Hmm.' He nodded in a way which was beginning to irritate. 'Checked that out when we got the initial report. Most of the buildings here follow a theme. A quirk of the developer, it seems.'

Blue and white tape marked the secure area of the crime scene, and we ducked beneath it as we made our way from the reception area and up the stairs to the office where the body lay. The victim had been identified as Michael Partridge, partner in the firm. The scene was a fairly simple one – he was face down in a pool of blood which had dried overnight. The wound to the back of his head was severe, and his hair was caked with a thick stream of blood which had partially obscured the right hand side of his face. This was a messy one. The body, though, was not our priority. Mavis Smith, the cleaner, had been waiting since seven to tell someone what she knew, and, leaving Parker to make what he could of the crime scene, I headed off back downstairs to a side office where the unfortunate woman sat with one of the division's uniform PCs. She stood and saluted as I entered.

'Good morning, sir.' She snapped to attention.

''Morning, Constable - ' I smiled.

'Watts, sir. Helen Watts.'

'At ease, Watts, before you strain something.' It was a weak attempt at humour, but it seemed to do the trick. I turned to Mavis

Smith, sat down at her side and smiled again. The woman was clearly still in a state of shock, and getting any useful information out of her at this point was going to be problematic, at the very least. Still, I persisted and did manage to get some sense of what she had been through since coming into the premises the previous evening.

'So, you worked a split shift, Mavis?'

'Yes, inspector,' she replied, still wiping the tears from her eyes. 'I do the majority of the cleaning between five and eight in the evening and catch up with the reception area the following morning just before people arrive for work.'

'According to what you told one of the officers earlier, you heard raised voices late on last night. Is that correct?' I looked up from Parker's notebook.

'I did, but they were always arguing about something.'

'That would be Mr Partridge and … ?'

'Mr Mason, Robert Mason, they're the two partners. It wasn't always so loud, though, and I try not to pay much attention. I left at the usual time, and they were still going on at each other. Must have been for over half-an-hour this time, and it didn't seem to be ending any time soon.'

'Have you seen Mr Mason at all this morning?'

'No, and that's quite unusual. They're both here before I start the morning hour – I finish at eight – but I never thought it would come to this.'

'All right, Mavis.' I smiled. 'Let's leave it there for the moment, but I may need to talk to you again, so make sure that PC Watts has a note of your address.'

2

Having interviewed the only person on-site at the time of the discovery of the body, Steve Parker and I now focussed on the steady stream of employees who were beginning to arrive for their day's work. Once the process of taking down their details and sending them home was almost complete, we had a list of twenty-three potential suspects. Oddly, Robert Mason was not amongst them. I looked up at Parker, but he beat me to the punch.

'See anything odd, guv?'

'Yes, Mason's not here today.' I frowned. 'Wonder why that could be. Is the secretary still here?'

'She is – I saw her a few minutes ago,' he replied. 'I asked her for a complete list of anyone leaving the firm on less than amiable terms over the past year. She should be in her office.' We found Marisa Singleton going through the employee files, and she turned as we approached the open door. Her hands were shaking, and she was fighting hard to hold back the tears. This would require careful handling.

'Ms Singleton, I'm Detective Inspector Mellors. I think you've already met my DS. Could I have a contact address for Robert Mason, please?'

'Yes, that's in my desk diary.' She moved round to the desk on the other side of the room and opened a leather-bound book. 'Here, please help yourself while I finish off over there.' Having written Mason's address and telephone number in my notebook, I sat on the edge of the desk and waited for her to complete the task set by Parker. She closed the filing cabinet, locked it and turned to face the two of us.

'Ms Singleton, you are the company secretary?'

'Yes, and PA to both of the partners. We're a small company right now, and it suits the needs of the firm to combine both positions.'

'I see. So, you would be aware of any conflicts between Mr Partridge and Mr Mason.' I left this as a statement, thus removing from her any temptation to lie.

'I'm privy to the company plans, yes.'

'That's not what I said.' I stared at her. 'Let me put it another way: was there any part of the company plan which was causing friction between them?' She looked from me to Parker and back. She sat down, sighed, and opened up. The company, it would seem, was in the process of pioneering a revolutionary new microchip with the potential to catapult computer processing speed into a previously unanticipated dimension. In short, all current versions of microchip technology would be rendered obsolete overnight.

'But surely,' I continued, nonplussed, 'wouldn't this be a cause for celebration?'

'Inspector, I know only what I've already said. The details of the project are way beyond my understanding, but I'm aware that Mr Mason was keen on taking up an offer from one of the major American players in the industry.'

'And Mr Partridge?' I pushed the issue further.

'Michael thought that the offer should be rejected. They both own fifty percent of the company shares, and he thought that they should develop the new software together. It was starting to cause some terrible rows.'

'I see. Where is Mr Mason right now?'

'I've no idea. He's normally in well before the rest of us – apart from Michael, that is.'

'All right. Let's leave it there, but we will need to talk to you again. For the moment, go home; the whole site is a crime scene, and we need to examine the entire property before it can be re-opened.'

Parker and I remained in the office after she and the rest of the workforce had been cleared from the site. We now had a viable suspect. Mason had motive, opportunity and, if the murder weapon could be found, potentially the means, to kill his partner. He could then assume Partridge's share of the company and sell out to the American bidder. The only question remaining was: Where was he? That thought was to be consigned to the backburner by a call from Harry Bostock. We were required at the lab to check out an interesting forensic development.

'Okay, Harry, where's the fire?' I smiled – it was becoming a habit right now. I was keen to get home some time today to see my little girl for the first time in a week.

'Are all you plain clothes people funny, or is it just you?' he growled. I gave up on the levity.

'We're here. What have you got?'

'Scrapings.' He nodded towards a table where his samples had been stored. 'You know, killers are remarkably stupid when it comes to the leaving of trace evidence. This' - he held up a test tube - 'was taken from beneath our victim's fingernails.'

'You got a DNA match? That was fast!' I tensed, a sense of excitement growing for the first time today. Maybe this was going to be one of those famous 'open and closed' cases.

'Indeed. I have my ways and means.' He glowed and smiled for the first time in a thousand years. 'This young woman' - he handed me one of our own files - 'was arrested for shoplifting a year ago in Sainsbury's. Just opposite your HQ, isn't it?'

'Heather Miller.' I read the front sheet. 'Wait a minute. Steve' - I turned to my DS - 'where's that list of ex-employees that Marisa Singleton gave us?'

'Here, guv.' He pulled it from an inside pocket. 'There she is.' He pointed half way down the sheet. 'Dismissed for theft – yesterday! They had to call us out when she flipped, but that was the end of it.'

'That's a turn-up, and just when I thought we had someone else in the frame. Is there an address on that sheet?'

'There is.'

'Time we paid her a visit, then.' I turned to Bostock. 'Thanks, Harry, you're a star.'

I pretended not to hear the snort of derision as we left the lab and headed back to my car. Heather Miller lived in Heanor. Ten minutes later, we were outside her terraced home on Derby Road.

'Yeah?' A bleary-eyed young woman in her mid-twenties tried to focus on our ID cards as we stood outside her front door. 'What do you want?'

'Inside would be better, Ms Miller.' I said. 'Unless, that is, you want the entire street to hear what we have to say.' She stepped aside and closed the door behind us. The house was dark, cold and damp. I guessed that the gas and electricity had been cut off, and, as we walked down the hall to a sitting room at the back of the property, she took out a pack of filter-tips and lit up. So much for the priorities of life. I looked at the glowing cigarette.

'I can smoke in my own home, and you can clear off if you don't like it,' she growled.

'I'll come straight to the point,' I said, waving away a thick cloud of bluish smoke. 'Where were you between ten and midnight last night?'

'Why? What's that to you?'

'You've just left PM Micro Electronics, haven't you?' She snapped out of her semi-comatose state as though I'd shot a bolt of electricity through her. Ironic in the circumstances, as she didn't seem to be able to afford her own. Her face set, as the recollection of the dismissal came sharply to the forefront of her memory. Stubbing out the cigarette, she stomped up to me.

'What's that git, Partridge, been sayin' now?' she yelled. I wiped her spittle from my jacket and pushed her away.

'Not a word. You see, he's dead.'

'Dead?' Miller's voice suddenly lost all of its venom.

'Dead, and with your DNA underneath his fingernails! That's a nasty scratch on your wrist.' I pointed to her right arm, and she covered the scar with her hand. 'Where did you get it?'

'Partridge!' she snapped. 'I didn't kill him, though. He fired me yesterday 'cos somebody told him I'd nicked some stuff from the factory. I lost it and went for him. Must've caught me on the wrist when they pulled me off him.'

'Where were you last night?' It was my turn to step forward, and she retreated to the safety of an old worn armchair. She slumped into its depths, but her face remained set.

'Over the road at the Miners', and there's a shed-load of people who'll tell you the same. Didn't leave there until chucking-out time; I was drunk, and three of them helped me into the house – go and check!' Her anger had returned and, faced with a convincing story, Parker and I set out across the Derby Road to the Miners' Arms, one of the two remaining public houses in that part of Heanor. Our presence at the pub killed all conversation in the bar stone dead, and the landlord, Stanley Nelson according to the licensee name above the door, waved us through the bar hatch and into the private quarters to the rear of the property.

3

'Yes, she was here all evening from about eight onwards.' Nelson was calm and assured. There was nothing in his demeanour to suggest that he was covering for Miller.

'How can you be so sure?' I asked. 'Could she have left, even for an hour, without you noticing?'

'Not a chance.' The landlord folded his arms. 'Darts night, see? Semi-final for the women's team, and Heather's our best player. We won hands down, and she was perfect in every match she played. When she wasn't at the oche, she was propping up the bar.'

'I suppose there'll be a stack of witnesses to provide an alibi,' Parker remarked.

'Some of them are out there if you want to ask. She's a very popular regular, and it'd be a surprise if she wasn't here, especially on a night like last night.'

We left the Miners' Arms suddenly deflated. Having spoken to those in the pub, we had to accept that Miller's alibi was as solid as a rock, and we were now forced to return to our first suspect, Robert Mason. His address put him on the other side of Derby, in Allestree. With the day closing in on us, it was almost five before we arrived outside the property on Birchover Way, and the house was in darkness. Repeated knocking at the front door brought no response, but a neighbour walking a dog provided us with some interesting information as we left and closed the front gate.

'Robert left in a bit of a hurry late last night.'

'How late, Mr Johnson?' Tony Johnson and his wife had been returning from the Markeaton Hotel, following an evening with friends, and had seen Mason's BMW speeding away from the area.

'It would be around eleven, I think,' he said. 'I'm sure about that, because, although I waved to him, he totally ignored both of us – most unusual. I remember looking at my watch and thinking that it was so late for him to be going out; he's a bit of a home bird. Didn't see his wife in the car, though.'

'There's a Mrs Mason?' Parker looked up from his notebook.

'Yes. They've been married a couple of years. Nice couple, and he's a very successful businessman, I've heard.'

'Thank you, Mr Johnson. You've been very helpful. If you remember anything else, there's my number at the bottom of the card.' I handed him one of the business-cards that we're all obliged to keep nowadays, and he continued on his way home.

'Interesting,' Parker said. 'Time to put out an alert? We've got his details.'

'Get on to it now, Steve.' We got back into the car. 'I don't want this guy getting out of the county.'

Parker was on his mobile as I spoke, and, by the time we arrived back at Ripley HQ, every force in the East Midlands was on the lookout for Mason. It wasn't long before we got the vital breakthrough – Mason's BMW had been pulled over the previous evening on the A38 south of Branston. Uniform had stopped and breathalysed him – he had been over the limit and was now in custody at Burton police station off Horninglow Street. Maybe now I could smile. I looked at my watch and sighed – *another* evening when I'd miss my little girl's bedtime. A call to the desk sergeant ensured that he'd be waiting to see us by the time we'd made the hour's trip to the Staffordshire station.

'Mr Mason.' I was out of smiles – it was too late in the day. 'DI Mellors and DS Parker from Ripley. In a bit of a hurry last night, were you?' Mason looked and sounded rough – a night in police cells will do that to you. He'd received a call from one of our patrols the previous evening, he said. His wife had been on an evening out with work colleagues and had been involved in a nasty collision with another vehicle.

'Marion, my wife, wasn't badly hurt: just a few bruises, but I panicked, grabbed my car keys and headed off for the crash site. Never thought about the beer I'd drunk.'

'How unfortunate,' Parker said. 'What time did you get that call, sir?'

'Around eleven – you can check with your blokes. I got there at about half-past.'

'Speeding as well as drinking, then?' I asked.

'Wouldn't you?' He frowned. 'Look, this can't be just about a drink/drive charge, can it? Two of you out here at this hour, just for me?'

'No,' I replied. 'It's much more serious. Your partner, Michael Partridge, has been found dead at your Heanor site. I understand the two of you had a serious row yesterday.'

'Dead? Michael? But how?' Mason looked genuinely surprised, but I'd seen enough of that in my time on the force and dismissed it for the moment.

'My sergeant and I were wondering whether you could tell us that.'

'Me? I didn't kill him.' He looked stunned at the accusation. 'I left the place at around seven thirty, and he was alive then. The cleaner was still there – ask her.'

'We did, sir.' Parker took up the conversation. 'It was she who told us about the row. Get out of hand, did it? It was a very nasty injury. What was it that you hit him with?' Mason's protestations of innocence continued, and we were unable to shake his story. I had to admit that the timings, allowing for his trip into Staffordshire, would have been very tight. Still, he was our only suspect for the moment, so we left him to stew at the station. The desk sergeant was under instructions not to release him without my permission. We got back to Ripley to find a note from the front desk waiting for us. Mavis Smith, the cleaner mentioned by Mason, and our first witness, had apparently remembered something. The kettle had just boiled when we arrived at her house in Loscoe.

'I completely forgot in all the confusion this morning, inspector,' she said. 'Would you and your sergeant like some tea?'

'Love one, please, Mrs Smith.' We sat down. 'What was it that you remembered?'

'Well, you notice things when you do the work that I do, and, as I clean it every day, it seemed odd that it wasn't there this morning.'

'I'm sorry, you'll have to explain. What was it that you couldn't find?'

'The award.' She smiled. 'The one they won last year. Mr Partridge was ever so proud of it, and it was on the reception desk where everyone coming in and out could see it.'

'Award?' I leaned forward. 'What kind of award?'

'Oh, now let me see if I can remember what it said on it.' She took a sip from her cup and suddenly brightened. 'Chamber of Commerce, it said. Can't remember much more than that. Heavy-looking glass thing it was – fingerprints all over it. I was always having to clean them off.' A sudden thought hit me.

'But you couldn't have cleaned it today, could you?'

'No,' she said. 'Makes me cross, does that; I always take a pride in what I do.'

With Mavis Smith unable to add anything further, we left and got back in the car. Whoever had handled the award last would have left their prints on it, and a process of elimination should give us a break in the case. I was starting to see the light and was now certain that I knew who had killed Michael Partridge. I looked at my watch and cursed: late home once again.

'We'll call it a day now, Steve.' I sighed. 'I'll be a little late in tomorrow; there's a call I have to make and I'll tell you about it when I get in.'

Carol, my wife, was still up when I arrived home. Unlike many wives in the force, she understood clearly the pressures of the job and the number of times it invaded our private lives. She was curled up with a book on the sofa as I came into the lounge. Her smile lit up an otherwise dreary day, and we made our way to the kitchen.

'Molly was asking when you'd be home,' she said without reproach. 'Bedtime stories aren't the same from me; she says I don't tell them right.'

'Sorry, love.' I took the coffee she'd made and sat down. 'We've almost got this case cracked, so I should be home in time on Christmas Eve, at least.'

'Hope so.' She smiled. 'Our little girl has a special present for her daddy – she chose it herself and wrote a letter to Santa telling him exactly what it was.'

4

I left the headquarters of the Chamber of Commerce on Derby's Victoria Way with a confidence in my step. The parcel in my hand could well be the final piece in the jigsaw which would expose the killer of Michael Partridge. Steve Parker was waiting eagerly as I stepped into the office and smiled broadly when I explained the plan I'd hatched the previous day.

'Ring Marisa Singleton, Steve, and ask her to meet us at Pear Tree House. Tell her to bring her keys with her and explain that we need another look at the personnel records she keeps.' Singleton was outside the police-cordon as we arrived in Heanor. Once inside the premises, she and Parker went directly to her office, and she unlocked the cabinet whilst I had a word with the uniformed officer outside the main entrance.

'You said it was urgent, inspector,' she said as I entered the room. 'Where do you want to begin?'

'Is Robert Mason's file in there?' I asked.

'Yes: they all are; there are no exceptions for status.' She seemed anxious. 'I'll get it for you.' She turned back from the cabinet. 'Have you arrested him?'

'For what?' Parker interrupted.

'Murder.' She bit her tongue at the slip.

'Why would we do that when he wasn't even here at the time Mr Partridge was killed?' Her face flushed, and she backed away. There was a knock at the door, and the uniformed PC I'd spoken to earlier came into the room. I looked his way and raised my eyebrows, ensuring that Singleton saw every gesture.

'Yes, Pollard?'

'Where you said it would be, sir.'

'Thank you, constable.' I took the polythene bag from him, and he left. Singleton exploded.

'How did you get into my car!?' she yelled, stepping forward and reaching out for the bag.

'Sit down!' I shouted, and she backed away. 'Steve' - I turned to Parker - 'go and take a look in Ms Singleton's vehicle.' I held out my hand. 'Keys, please, Marisa.'

The two of us waited in total silence as Parker carried out the task which would close the trap around Partridge's PA. It must have seemed an age to her before he returned with the award. Twelve inches by six and half-an-inch thick – it was a formidable weapon.

'There's blood on one of the corners, guv.' He handed it to me, and Singleton collapsed into a chair at the side of the cabinet.

'Why, Marisa?' I asked.

'He was dumping me,' she explained between sobs. 'We'd been together for over a year, and suddenly, just as the firm is set to take off, he dumps me. I was so angry; I asked him why, but all he could do was laugh in my face. He said I wasn't the kind of woman he'd like to have on his arm in the places where he and Robert were going to be.'

'You were jealous of his success?'

'No!' she snapped, 'I loved him, but he didn't care about that. He turned to get himself a drink, and I grabbed the first thing I could.'

'The award.'

'Yes.' Her composure had returned. 'He'd fetched it up from reception during the day, and it was on his desk. He never saw me coming – I was so mad at him.'

'Why didn't you call for an ambulance? He could have still been alive.'

'I panicked. There was so much blood.' She said; her voice was beginning to break up again. 'I wrapped the award up and shoved it into the boot of my car. I was going to move it into Robert's BMW as soon as I could, but things moved too quickly.'

'And Heather Miller?' I asked. 'Was she your backup plan in case the ruse with Mason didn't work?'

'Miller? The thief in our despatch?' She looked surprised. 'That was nothing to do with me.'

We were done with Singleton. Once Harry Bostock had confirmed fingerprint and DNA evidence from the trophy, her confession would provide a watertight case. I was now left with just a couple of loose ends to tie up, and the Christmas holiday would be beckoning. It was early afternoon when I arrived at Birchover Way in Derby, and a relieved Robert Mason ushered me into his lounge, where his wife sat resting after her ordeal in the accident.

'It's really all over, is it?' he asked.

'Yes. We have a confession from Marisa Singleton and evidence from the weapon which will convict her. There are a couple of things that I'd like to ask you, though.'

'Fire away,' he replied. 'We're both just relieved that it's all behind us.'

'Now that Michael's gone, what will happen to the company? I gather you had a great opportunity on the horizon.'

'It's still there – I spoke to the Americans as soon as I got here and explained what had happened to Mike. We'll be okay; the software was a joint project, and we both knew all of the ins and outs of it. They've actually upped their offer now that I'm on my own, so, sad as it may seem, there's a silver lining at the end of it. What was the other matter?'

'Heather Miller.'

'Ahh, the woman Michael sacked for pilfering?'

'That's the one. I spoke to the landlord at her local, where she's a bit of a local star in the darts team. He was amazed that she'd been dismissed. Told me that she'd stood in behind the bar at The Miner's Arms on a number of occasions, and that nothing had gone missing.'

'So, what are you suggesting, inspector?'

'The woman's strapped for cash – I've seen where she lives. It may be in your interest to offer her the job back before she takes it into her head to sue you for unfair dismissal.'

'You may have a point there, but what about the stuff that went missing?'

'Check your stocks first and then decide whether there might be someone else on the premises with a grudge against her. In any case, you could think about making some kind of ex-gratia payment to her for the inconvenience the firm has caused. I'm sure that she has some bills which need paying.'

'I'll do that, thanks. Did you really think that I could have killed Michael? We argued, it's true, but we've been friends since our university days.'

'It's my job to suspect everyone, Mr Mason: there's nothing personal in it.'

5

There was just one more call to make before I caught up with Steve Parker back at Ripley, and I was knocking on the door of Heather Miller's home on Derby Road in Heanor a little after three that afternoon. The face which greeted me had not changed significantly since Steve and I questioned her previously, and I hadn't had a chance to explain the reason for my call before I was greeted with a truculent demand.

'What d'you want this time, copper?'

'Good afternoon to you too, Ms Miller. Don't worry, this isn't an official visit - I have some good news.' Her face softened slightly, and she frowned in puzzlement.

'What could you possibly say to me that would be good news?'

'Well, for starters, I think you'll find that your job at the electronics company is there for you to return to. Shouldn't be surprised if Robert Mason has some apologetic words to say into the bargain. Go easy on him; you're not the only one who's had a rough time of it for the past few days.'

'My job? I don't have one: they fired me on some trumped-up charge.'

'Mr Mason has been - let's say – encouraged to see the light. Your friendly landlord at the Miner's Arms was glowing in his praise of your honesty; I merely passed the sentiments on.' She was wavering – I went in for the kill. 'What could you possibly have to lose? If there really is a thief at PM Micro Electronics, your return will certainly put the wind up them. Keep a lookout for anyone leaving in the next week or so.'

I left her standing there on the doorstep. I really did hope that she took the advice, but I had little time to spare now, if I were to make the deadline for Molly's Christmas Eve. Hopes were all but dashed on my return to Ripley by Parker's greeting as I stepped inside the door.

'Chief Super wants to see the two of us upstairs.' He had lost his trademark grin, and I knew we were both in for a long session. Much as I appreciate that the top brass need to know, it could surely have waited until after the holiday. I was not wrong. The actual congratulations on a job well done took less than ten minutes; the remainder of the hour and a half was spent in so much hackneyed lecturing that I can't remember any of it. By the time we got out of there, it was way past my little girl's bedtime. With all hope of seeing her before she went to sleep lost, I called in at the lab just as Harry Bostock was leaving. He seemed pleased to see me for a change.

'Just the chap.' He smiled – that worried me. 'I found DNA traces on that award thing, and they matched the swab you took from that Singleton woman, so I suppose that's your open and shut case for you. Goodnight.'

With all loose ends now tied up, I made my way to the exit. Pulling out of Wyatt's Way, I turned into Sainsbury's – a box of chocolates for the wife and a bottle between the two of us would round the day off nicely. The store was winding down for the night as I got out of the car. I smiled at the sign over the entrance; they'd really gone to town this year – *'Santa in his Grotto'*, it read, *'Make Your Dream Come True'*. The man himself was just leaving as I approached and we smiled at each other – two professionals on the last leg of their day.

'Busy time?' I smiled as we met.

'Isn't it always?' he replied, passing to my right. He stopped suddenly. 'Oh, I almost forgot: Merry Christmas.' Reaching into one of the deep pockets on his tunic, he pulled out a small cube-shaped parcel wrapped in brightly-coloured paper. His full white beard blew in the wind, and I looked down in surprise at the gift. When I looked up again, he was gone, and yet my glance away could have only been for a matter of seconds. I frowned as I unwrapped the gift. It was a small blue box covered in a kind of suede material; I flipped open the lid and pulled out a small card. Leaning against one of the floodlight-pylons, I held my breath as I read my daughter's large round script. *'I asked Santa to get you these, and he said that he'd make sure that you got them in time – Love, Molly'*. We'd laughed about the cufflinks in the shape of a policeman's hat when we saw them in Derby, and I now recall Carol telling her to write to Santa Claus. The booming laughter echoing around the empty car park sent a shiver down my spine.

'Merry Christmas,' I whispered.

White Christmas Bullet
James McCarthy

The flickering Christmas lights were distracting him, and he hoped the girl dressed as Santa Claus handing out fliers wouldn't walk into his line of fire. He hesitated a second and then squeezed the trigger. He heard a loud click, and instinctively held his breath and waited for the flash and bang. Nothing happened. This was a practice-run while he waited for the real target, not yet due.

He had rested the barrel of the sniper rifle on the window-ledge of the hotel room twenty stories up and trained it through the telescopic sights on the door of Starbucks across the street. For this dry run, he aimed at the bald head of a man entering the coffee shop. He laid the gun on the table, closed the window and took two bullets from his pocket to load it. He had bought it in a gun-shop specialising in used weapons two blocks away less than an hour ago.

'Happy Holiday,' the sales assistant said. After that, it was a straightforward transaction: sign a fictitious name on the dotted line and away you go, no questions asked. He hadn't used his own name for so long that he had almost forgotten it - and the past that went with it.

He had concerns about the gun: if it were damaged, it could kill him on Christmas Eve. Anyway, he wasn't expecting any presents. He would have liked the opportunity to test-fire it, to see whether it worked. Gunsmiths checking firearms hold them in a vice, attach a cord to the trigger and yank on it. Either the gun fires or it explodes, the latter being preferable to blowing up in somebody's face. This type of test wasn't a choice for him; he didn't have the time or the facilities. He would have to chance it: taking risks was now part of his life, and he was still here. Another concern was the accuracy of the gun: with the number of Christmas revellers going in and out of Starbucks, he could easily take out an innocent person. He could take only one shot: the flash from his second shot would give his position away to the people in the street; they would no doubt call the cops. The hotel had only two exits, and, if he were surrounded by armed cops, it could prove difficult to escape.

A piece of paper fell to the floor. He picked it up: he didn't intend to leave trace. It was unwise to do that with all the modern detecting equipment about. He recognised the scrap of paper immediately: it was a page of the *Enquirer*. He didn't normally read it, but, in passing a New York news-stand, he glanced at the back page, and he knew he had to buy it. He opened it now, but he didn't reread all of it, only the main part.

> The Irish People don't deserve the mess the country is in, thanks to unscrupulous politicians, developers and bankers. They must pay. We want to hear from you, if you have military experience, or if you are a target shooter. Contact us, the Vigilantes of Irish Americans (VIA), by phone, text or e-mail. Confidentiality guaranteed. There is an excellent compensation packet for the right person.

The rest of the message, which had included the contact information, he had torn off, but that didn't matter as he had committed it to memory. At first, he thought it might be a joke, but it wasn't. The advert also appeared for a short time on twitter and Face Book and every other social site on the internet before they took it down. He applied for the job by e-mail, and they hired him. That explains why he was here in a tough neighbourhood of Chicago waiting in a rent-by-the-hour hotel where even the Christmas buntings are cheap and gaudy. He guessed his unknown employers were mainly expats. His pay for this job they deposited in a security box at Union Station, and they posted the key to him. He gave a station vagrant one hundred dollars to get it for him while he hid behind a pillar. Any sign of trouble and he would have quickly faded into the crowd. No one appeared, and the vagrant delivered the bag to him. The amount in hard cash was correct, but he would have carried out this mission for nothing for his country. He always needed a cause, and he thought of himself as a true patriot. If the cause proved bogus, then he would turn against it with the same fervour with which he joined it: his conscience demanded no less.

He didn't load the gun. The Republican brotherhood trained their volunteers well, instilling in them the maxim that a loaded gun is a dangerous weapon. They were normally not armed, the one exception being a volunteer on active service. Well, he could debate with himself whether this was currently the case, but he didn't have to. This to him was a just cause. When he was with the American Special Forces, they mostly carried arms of some sort, but that was another story.

He sat on the bed, took the gun apart and used a tin of Nugget Polish to darken the barrel, to stop the daylight reflecting on it. A snore reminded him there was another person in the toilet. He had forgotten about her. Knowing the hotel catered for special women and their clients, he thought it would look suspicious to the desk clerk if he booked in without an escort. He might think he was a terrorist placing a bomb and call the cops, and that was something he didn't want. He agreed a price and hired the first woman that accosted him on the street for a day's escort work. She looked grotesque dressed as Father Christmas. He got up from the bed and walked quietly over to the toilet and looked inside. She was sitting on the seat asleep with a bottle of Jack Daniels - a Christmas logo on the front of it - lying half empty on the floor. He picked up her mobile phone from beside her on the washbasin, closed the door and pushed the outside bolt into place. He needn't worry further about her upsetting his plans.

He had carried out surveillance on the target for weeks, and his hit was a man of habit, slavishly following the same pattern each day. He and his presence at the café across the street at 3.00 p.m. were almost a certainty, unless he changed his routine for the Christmas holiday. That was part of the uncertainty of being a hired gun.

'Hi, honey, Happy Holiday. I ain't got my cell with me to call my man. I got to get outa here.' He didn't expect to hear that. She mustn't be as drunk as he thought, and a crazed pimp looking for one of his women wasn't something he needed.

'Soon: that's what I paid you for.'

'Honey, I thought we were going to have some action. This is worse than the state pen, except there ain't no bitches in here. Ye got to let me out.'

'OK.' He opened the bathroom door. She sat slumped sideways on the toilet seat with her Santa hat hanging half off her head. To make her more comfortable, he pushed the chair with broken springs from the bedroom into the toilet. It was a tight fit between the cistern and the bidet, but she would be more stable sitting on it. He took her glass. Outside in the bedroom, he poured in some Rohypnol he had bought on the internet. The other choice they offered was ketamine, but he hadn't heard of it before, so he decided not to order it. They hadn't included dosage instructions for the Rohypnol, so he poured out what he considered was a large dessert-spoonful into the glass. He swirled it round, colourless and odourless, and it slowly dissolved in the Jack Daniels. 'Drink this, it'll make you feel better.' He handed her the glass.

'Thanks, honey. Happy Holiday! When do we get down to business?'

'Later.' He stood there while she emptied the glass, and he poured out some more whiskey for her. This dose would get her over, and he hoped he hadn't exceeded the amount. A dead prostitute on Christmas Eve was not part of his action-plan. He didn't have long to wait until she became groggy and then passed out. He locked the bathroom door as before, and this time he could forget about her and concentrate on the job in hand. He checked his watch: there was still an hour to wait, and, apart from the strangled hum of the broken air-conditioner, there was no sound in the room. He was about to lie down on the bed when he remembered there was an epidemic of bed-bugs in hotels in the large cities in the US. It was difficult to imagine that a country that could send men to the moon and back couldn't eradicate one of man's smallest pests, but that isn't the whole story. Fleas, according to the article he read, are extraordinary creations of nature that live on human blood. He could recall verbatim the text, the result of having to read and remember it for his civil engineering course, but that was so long ago. He was regrettably a different person now. This hotel, if one could call it that, had probably an infestation of fleas and 'roaches crawling all over it. He twitched as he imagined there were fleas crawling all over his back and along the nape of his neck, but, in reality, that was hardly likely. When he got back to his other hotel, his first mission would be to take a hot bath and get rid of his imaginary parasites. The clothes he was wearing would have to go as well. He checked the bottom of his fishing rucksack to see if they were crawling on it. Good Lord, he was developing a flea phobia!

He removed the canvas seat attached to the backpack, placed it in front of the window and sat on it. He slid open the window-sash, rested the rifle across his knees and tried to relax while he waited. The hotel tannoy burst into sound with 'White Christmas'.

Punctually at three o'clock, the taxi, decorated with Christmas streamers, pulled up outside Starbucks, and his target, with a glamorous female companion, not his wife, stepped out, both laughing and wearing Santa hats. His research had shown that this man owned penthouses in the major cities like New York, Washington and Chicago. Allegedly, this woman travelling with him from city to city was his secretary, but the gossip surrounding them suggested otherwise: a mistress, perhaps? Then the voice inside his head started up. It was as if somebody outside was shouting to him, 'Kill, kill, kill them all.' He pressed his hand hard against his temples, but he couldn't squeeze this voice quiet. He had to wait thirty seconds until it stopped of its own accord, and that seemed like for ever. Recently it was becoming a more regular occurrence. In anger, he kicked the seat out of his way, stretched out on the floor and sighted the rifle on his target. He aimed for a spot of grey hair showing under the Santa hat just above his left temple, waited for a second. As the man turned his head towards him, he squeezed the trigger. The bullet hit in the centre of his forehead. It went through his skull and emerged from the back of his head, spewing out a mixture of blood and brain-matter. His Santa hat fell off as he dropped to the pavement and rolled over in the snow. A splatter of blood landed on the woman's white linen dress, and, bewildered, she stared down at it and screamed.

There was no time to waste. He banged the window shut and started to disassemble the rifle, but he didn't get far before a noisy commotion started outside the bedroom door. Suddenly, an obese black man dressed as Santa Claus burst in brandishing a knife and shouting,

'Where's my woman?' He turned sideways as the man rushed at him. That saved his life, the blade went through his bicep rather than his chest. He didn't have time to feel pain, and, in one well-rehearsed movement, he brought the rifle butt up with force and connected with the knifeman's jaw. The knifeman dropped like a stone, and, to judge from the crack of breaking bone, his jaw had fractured. As his training kicked in, the sniper didn't hesitate: he grabbed the knife-handle and tugged the blade free. The pain was horrendous, and he sat down heavily on the floor before he collapsed. He wasn't completely out, just a bit woozy, similar to the feeling he had when he had a wisdom-tooth extracted under conscious sedation. He took in the scene in slow motion, the blood from his arm running down the floor under the outstretched hand of the unconscious pimp and the constant snoring from the bathroom. The need to sleep was almost overwhelming, but he knew he couldn't let that happen; he would have to get out of there. He kept trying to breathe deeply, in for five, out for eight, but that was making him sleepier. He was drifting. During his training with the Marines, he survived the ordeal of remaining awake and functioning for seventy-two hours. It was a make-or-break test for the trainees; a trial of mind over matter using will-power alone. Those that failed returned to their units, and those that remained became fully-fledged marines.

He called on that will-power now and, with a big effort, stood up, supporting himself against the back of the only chair remaining in the room. He reached across to his rucksack and, with his good hand, took out a roll of duct-tape. Holding the end of the tape in his teeth, he tore off a long strip and wrapped it tightly around the wound. As a tourniquet, it stopped the blood flowing down his arm. He came prepared for all exigencies and, blessed with strong teeth, he used them to open the bottle of bleach he took from his backpack. He poured it over the blood trail on the floor and wiped it with a cloth. Even the best modern technology couldn't extract any of his DNA from the residue left on the floor. He put the empty bleach bottle and the dirty rag back into the haversack. He removed the pimp's Santa suit and put it on. With all the Santas walking about, he could easily merge into the crowd. Almost as an afterthought, he took out the rusty handcuffs he had bought at a lawn sale. Made from wrought iron by a blacksmith long dead, they were, according to the seller, owned by his great-grandfather and used on a slave-plantation in the south. He hauled the pimp across the floor to the radiator and handcuffed him to the feed-pipe. He would have liked to keep the handcuffs, as they were a genuine example of American memorabilia, but at least he was putting them to good use. It would take ages to free the pimp from the pipe. They would have to dismantle part of the central heating to release him. He hoisted the haversack on to his good shoulder and headed for stairs leading to the fire-escape. The desk clerk was coming up to meet him.

'Ho, ho, ho, Happy Holiday,' he said, slipping easily into the Santa role.

'What was the shouting about up here?' asked the clerk, sounding breathless from climbing up the stairs. Street-smart, he didn't take the lift where he could have come face-to-face with a killer.

'Ho, ho, ho, nothing to worry about: it was from outside on the pavement.'

'That's what I thought, but it's my job to find out. Happy Holiday,' said the clerk, sounding relieved. Already he had started back down the stairs to his desk. He wouldn't be doing this job if he weren't heavily in debt to the mob for crack they supplied, which he couldn't ever hope to pay for. It was this way or a concrete coffin.

The sniper stopped inside the back door of the hotel to don dark glasses and to pull down his Santa hat over his eyes before stepping into the street. He didn't want the security cameras to get anything but a Santa image of him. He walked as quickly as he could for two blocks to the gun shop where he had purchased the sniper-rifle. He recognised the counter assistant.

'I bought this rifle from you a few hours ago - '

'Happy Holiday. I have no recollection of that, we see so many customers. What do you want to do with the rifle: sell it?'

'Sell it.' The price offered was less than half of what he paid for it, but he was in no fit state to bargain. He took the money and left. He discarded the Santa suit, his blood-stained gloves, boiler-suit and rucksack in a dumpster, before walking for another block to where he had parked his hire-car. He wasn't feeling good as he nosed the car into the traffic. He decided to follow the street signs to the Mercy Hospital where he parked in the visitors' car park and staggered into the reception area all decked out for Christmas. He waited in line for the triage-nurse.

'Happy Holiday,' she said without much conviction. 'I'm Nurse Anderson. What can we do for you today?'

'I got stabbed.'

'Where's the wound?'

'My arm: I've covered it with tape to stop the bleeding.'

'OK, name, address and social security number,' she said, pen poised over a clipboard. She wrote down the false details he gave her.

'How are you going to pay for your treatment: insurance?'

'No, cash, money up-front,' he said, using American speech. He remembered a saying from his youth, which was apt in this situation: 'When in Russia, do as the Russians do.' She pulled on protective gloves and cut away the duct-tape.

'You've a nasty wound here. I'll put on a temporary dressing until the doctor sees you.' He sat in the triage-area waiting to get called, and he almost didn't recognise the false name he had used when they came to it. He was using so many aliases nowadays, there was a real danger of permanently forgetting who he was.

'I'm Doctor Mitch. How did this happen?'

'I got mugged, but they didn't get my wallet.'

'Have you reported it to the cops?'

'Not yet.'

'Mm, I'll clean it up, and send a swab to the lab. It needs suturing. You've lost a lot of blood, and I'd recommend a transfusion. Are you allergic to any medicines?'

'I'm not allergic to any of them that I know of, but I'd like to pass on the transfusion.' With all the controversy over contaminated blood, he didn't want any of it to enter his veins, now or at any time, unless he was in danger of death, and he was a long way from that.

'OK, if that's your choice. We'll put you on antibiotics to prevent infection.'

The stitches going in were painful, and he gritted his teeth. It was a relief when it was over.

'Drink plenty liquid for the next few days, and it's important to rest your arm as much as you can. It should heal up OK, apart from leaving some scar-tissue, but you could see the plastic-surgeons at a later date to consider a skin-graft. Where will we send the lab report?'

'I'm here on a Christmas vacation, and I'll phone for the results. Thank you.' He paid his bill in the accounts department, and it was time to go. A choir of carol singers had gathered in the waiting area singing 'White Christmas'. He felt weak and light-headed driving back to his hotel, The Great Lakes, near the Chicago Tribune building. He drove to the rear car park of the hotel that is spread out over an acre of manicured green space with low boxwood borders. In the land of plenty, they didn't need high-rise car parks with lots of cheap prairie-land available. He parked in bay twenty-one and glanced up at the windows at the back of the hotel. He needed to make sure he could see the car from his bedroom window. If the cops were looking for him, they would first home in on his hire-car. He had not left any obvious trace, but he couldn't be sure that, with the sophisticated tracking equipment law-enforcement had nowadays, they wouldn't find him. The best he could hope for was that they wouldn't discover who did the shooting until a cold-case team worked it out fifty years from now.

He went straight to the swimming pool, not to swim but to make use of the swimming trunks, towels and bathrobe in Christmas scarlet colours that the hotel provided free for guests. He discarded his clothes in the rubbish bin to ensure he wasn't taking any fleas into his bedroom. He had a hot shower, which he felt would delouse him and banish his flea-phobia; he had enough on his mind without that. He took his room door smart-card from the hotel receptionist without speaking. It was better that she didn't know the guest in Room 3050 spoke with an Irish accent. He wasn't being paranoid: it was the approach he had used successfully for years to remain below the radar of the many groups determined to find him. He could make a list, but there was no need to. No one could feel secure with that lot on their tail. He could start with the police forces from both sides of the Irish border; go on to two extreme parliamentary factions in Northern Ireland; then the customs officials here in the US searching for illegal aliens; and, for good measure, he should add the not inconsequential resources of American law-enforcement. If they ever captured him, depending on the law in the particular state, he could face the death-penalty. He would accept that death if he had to, and he would feel his country was worth giving his life for. Maybe he was a misguided patriot, but he had little else in his life left to give him a purpose for living.

The hotel bedroom was clean but sparsely furnished, and new crisp sheets were a luxury he didn't very often have on his work sites. When he checked the car park through the bedroom window, it seemed deserted apart from the stationary rows of vehicles. He used his binoculars to make sure, but there was no activity anywhere near his hire-car. He felt satisfied with that for now. He always carried pocket-sized binoculars in the hope that one day they might warn him of approaching trouble. He didn't want to take any more tablets to get to sleep; he rang the desk clerk.

'Good evening, sir, and Happy Holiday. How can I help?'

'Send up a bottle of Irish whiskey to Room 3050 and put it on my bill.'

'Any particular brand, sir?'

'Jameson's. If you haven't got it, any Irish whiskey will do.'

'Will there be anything else?'

'A club sandwich.'

'Thank you sir.'

He left the phone down, and, in contrast to how he felt about them, he swallowed two tranquillisers. He shouldn't start drinking again, but he felt tired of being sober and, come to think of it, he felt tired of everything. His GP warned him not to take these tablets with alcohol, but who cared? Reality was slipping away from him, and he had enough insight left to know his behaviour was getting out of hand, bordering at times on the bizarre. However, this was the first time he had murdered anyone, although in his view it was a justified killing of a scumbag. He answered the knock on the door: a waiter stood there wearing a Christmas hat and carrying a tray with a bottle of Jameson whiskey and the sandwich he had ordered.

'Happy Holiday. Where shall I place it, sir?'

'On the table.' He gave the waiter a tip.

'Thank you, sir. Is there anything else?'

'No, thank you.' The waiter closed the door behind him. He poured himself a glass of whiskey, and, combined with the tablets, it might give him a night's sleep. That would be a first in a long time. He usually woke about 3.00 a.m. and couldn't sleep again without tranquillisers. He took off his jacket and shoes before lying down on the bed.

He slept throughout that afternoon and night and didn't wake until the following morning, when the sun lit up the south-facing window of his bedroom. He felt confused and for a minute couldn't work out why he was lying fully clothed on a bed in a strange room. The pain and stiffness in his arm brought him back to reality. They must have overmedicated him in the hospital. He couldn't remember when he had last slept like that, dead to the world. He swung his legs out of the bed on to the floor and stood up, cautiously testing his balance. He seemed all right apart from a non-functioning arm. He opened the bedroom door and, sure enough, the outside was garnished with a wreath of holly and ivy and a Happy Holiday sticker. The local newspapers and a copy of *Today in the USA* were neatly folded on a tray waiting for him to collect. Such service could only happen in America. He scanned the local papers first and a small paragraph on the second last page of one them reporting the shooting. He read it quickly concentrating on the main focus of the article.

The most likely reason for the murder of a businessman shot dead outside Starbucks on Rail Street yesterday afternoon was 'mistaken identity', a police spokesperson said. The dead man is a well-known realtor owning large condominiums in Chicago and other cities throughout the US. The police will not release his name until after they notify his family, who live in Europe.

The cops weren't looking for him; they would probably blame the mobs. That was a good result, although back in Ireland, because of the dead man's prominence in the financial collapse of the country, the media would show a deeper interest. They would speculate on who or what was behind his murder. That was not his problem: he had completed the task, and they had paid him for it. That was the American way, a good day's work for a good day's pay. He was trying to be flippant, but none of it sat easily on his mind. For what remained of his sanity he felt it essential not to dwell on it.

He picked up the brochure from the telephone table advertising an architectural tour of Chicago by boat: what civil and structural engineer could pass it up? His training in engineering was a long time ago, and unfortunately he never got a chance to practise his skills. With the assumed identities he was using, he probably never would. This sightseeing opportunity might not happen again for him, so he decided to take the tour. Out at Navy Pier, he boarded a boat decked out with lavish Christmas decorations for the short voyage that included dinner. He guessed the long line of people waiting were out-of-towners like himself. He read through the brochure and decided the port side was the best place to go as they travelled down the river to the lake. Two young women pushed in beside him on the rail. With plenty of viewing space further along the deck, it almost seemed as if they wanted to get near him.

'Sorry to crush you like this, but we're only here for two days, and we want to see everything,' said the blonde girl to his right. Surreptitiously he checked to make sure his wallet was still in his back pocket.

'That's OK. I think the best views are from this side,' he said, secretly wishing they had picked someone else to squash against the rail.

'I'm Brandy, and this is Norma. You're from Ireland, with an accent like that,' said the blonde girl.

'Yes, but I'm a long time out of it,' he said, not wanting to elaborate, which would involve rehashing the bogus past he had invented, telling people he had retired from active membership of the Irish Republican Brotherhood, employed now as a hit-man to eliminate some of Ireland's rogue-gallery. That would surely go down like a lead balloon.

'I just love the Irish brogue: it's so soft, I could listen to it all day. Norma and I are best friends for ever, and this is our first time away together. She's a widow, and I'm recently divorced. It's my first Christmas without my husband,' she said. It was typical of Americans telling a stranger within minutes of meeting their biggest secrets without embarrassment. Norma seemed the more reserved one, and she held out her hand awkwardly.

'Pleased to meet you,' she said. 'We're from North Carolina, and most people have only a hazy idea where that is.' He shook her hand.

'I know it well; that's where I have my swamp-logging and coal-mining business.'

'That's amazing, meeting someone from our home-state,' said Norma looking up at him, and, although she wasn't that small, he was towering over her.

'It would be a bigger coincidence if you lived in Edenton NC,' he said, aware that he was giving away more information than he normally did, but, on balance, it seemed like harmless chat.

'We don't. It's a big state. I run a model agency that I started years ago with my ex-husband. Brandy works with me,' said Norma, getting more talkative by the minute. Brandy was sussing out fellow travellers as if she were looking for someone.

'Oh, there's Chuck from the hotel. Excuse me, you two, I'm going over to talk to him.' She pulled away from the rail, and with a wave of her hand she left.

'You're the first model agency owner I've ever met,' he said, glad to have more room now that Brandy was gone.

'I could say the same. You're the first Irish swamp-logger and coal-mine owner I've met. Then again, I never meet loggers and coal-miners in the modelling business,' she said, smiling at the thought of it.

'Yes, some of my coal-miners and loggers would fit easily into the modelling business,' he said. They both laughed. He glanced at the map on the brochure to figure out where they were.

'What have you found?' she said, leaning over to look at the brochure.

'We are seeing several historical buildings on this tour, such as the NBC Tower, Tribune Building, Wrigley Building, John Hancock Centre, Sears Tower, and on it goes,' he said giving her the tour brochure. She looked through it for a few minutes.

'It would take me more than one tour to get all that into my head. Where are you staying in Chicago?' she asked, handing the booklet back to him

'In the Great Lakes Hotel,' he answered, again forgoing his usual caution of revealing little about himself.

'Isn't that a coincidence? We're staying there as well. Can I travel back with you? It would save time, rather than having to wait for a taxi,' she said.

'That's no problem,' he assured her.

'I don't see Brandy about. I'll give her a ring,' she added, taking her mobile phone from her bag. She walked away from him to make the call. That seemed unusual: they were hardly going to discuss something of National Importance.

'Brandy's going back with Chuck. He's from New York and seems a nice guy,' she commented, returning the phone to her handbag. The cruise finished at Navy Pier, and, going ashore, they passed under a mistletoe-arch held aloft by two young women dressed in mini-skirted Santa outfits. Laughing aloud, she gave him a peck on the cheek as they went under it.

He parked round the back of the hotel in the same lot as before and opened the door for her to get out. She seemed reluctant to move as if waiting for something or someone. The atmosphere between them had changed. She had suddenly became cold as if she were a different person. A limousine emerged from the side of the hotel where it was hidden from view. Highly ornate and with elaborate Christmas decorations, there was no mistaking it for anything else but a pimp-wagon. It screeched to a halt ahead of him. Armed with a machine-pistol, the pimp he had handcuffed to the heating pipes jumped out. Brandy, if indeed that was her name, waved and ran to the pimp to embrace him, shouting,

'I love my man.' When she looked back at him, her face was a mask of hate She spat out, 'Sucker, you've been had.' Too late he realised it had all been a set-up.

The bullets hit him in the chest, spinning him around before he dropped to the ground. He felt no pain, just numbness from the hole in his chest and warm sticky liquid dripping on to his hands. He knew it was blood. From a car that had just pulled into the car park, a woman dressed in Salvation Army black rushed over to him. She dropped to her knees and cradled his head in her arms.

'Do you accept Jesus Christ as your Lord and Saviour?' she asked softly, although there was urgency in her voice. It sounded to him like the voice of an angel coming from somewhere distant. He knew he was dying, but, if he needed confirmation, he had just got it. He had given up religion many years ago, but she had brought him back in his mind to his school days; but that was some time ago and far away. If only he could go back, start again, everything would be different. He would use his potential for good, and only good, to make the world a better place, but it was too late: there was no going back.

Then he remembered the Parable of the 'Prodigal Son'. In a voice faint and hoarse he said:

'I do.' In the same soft voice she asked him:

'What's your name?' Almost inaudible, he uttered his last word:

'It's - '

The Reading
Andrew D. Malloy

One

'I'd like to begin by thanking everyone for attending here today.' Frederick Peabody of Peabody, Stoughton and Harwood opened proceedings. He peered over the rim of his glasses at the five people seated in front of him. 'In my profession time is money - '

'And don't we know it.' Stray whisperings from one of the five stopped him dead. The lawyer's resultant expression suggested something offensive had suddenly attached itself to his top lip. He stabbed the offender through the heart – metaphorically, that is - and carried on.

' - therefore, it is my intention to proceed directly to the formal reading of the last will and testament of the late Richard Geoffrey Wilkinson.' Peabody lifted two brown envelopes from the desk, one in each hand. He held aloft the heavier-looking for all to see. 'This envelope contains Mr Wilkinson's detailed instructions as to the disposal of his estate. Mr Wilkinson personally handed it to me seven days before he passed away. I can confirm that I have no prior knowledge of its contents.' He pointed to a blob of red wax bearing the letters 'RGW' - Wilkinson's personal applied seal – which covered the opening. Then Peabody switched his attention to the other envelope. 'This envelope contained two prepared statements from Mr Wilkinson, the first of which resulted in our reading here today and the second of which I am about to reveal to you. Please note that the envelope itself was addressed as follows: 'For the sole attention of Mr Frederick Peabody of Peabody, Stoughton and Harwood, Solicitors, with the express instruction: to be opened exactly one year after my death'. Further to Mr Wilkinson's wishes, I can confirm that the envelope was duly opened by my own hand, seven days ago, on the 17th of

November, 2013, on the first anniversary of his death. The procedure took place here at the offices of Peabody, Stoughton and Harwood and under the supervision of my fellow-partners, Ms Helen Stoughton and Mr Percy Harwood.' Another belly-rumble from the gallery sounded as if it bore enough pent-up frustration to go round all five of them. The general feeling among the family, especially those with the smell of money in their nostrils, was that to have to wait a year to get to this point pretty well stank up the place.

Retired Judge Richard Wilkinson had never married. His only family had been a brother - also deceased - and five blood-relatives descended from both the brother and an uncle on his father's side. When his cancer had really taken hold, Wilkinson had to call in some favours to locate three of the five, before it was too late. The aggressive nature of the cancer meant that his master-plan almost died with him.

The second minor outburst provoked a reaction from Frederick Peabody similar to the previous one, then:

'Very well, then, we'll get right down to it, shall we?' Peabody forced a smile over his thin lips. He lifted the second statement and began: 'Statement prepared by Richard Geoffrey Wilkinson, signed and dated the 10th of November, 2012.'

> The fact that you are present for the reading of my last will and testament obviously means that I am no longer living among you. All of you were invited to attend my funeral service. For those who did take the time, I thank you. I expect you are all a little confused, upset even, at the length of time it has taken to arrive at this point.

More murmurings.

> The reason for the delay? Ironically, legal processes. Mr Peabody will explain the finer details later.

> As you know, in life I gained the reputation in my courtroom of never being one to suffer fools gladly. Many times during my legal career I felt that the law and its convoluted and often

divisive processes were the fools to be ungladly suffered. Of course, in life I would never have been prepared to utter such a statement, not even in private. Now, wherever I am, above or below, I am free to express an opinion not guided by oath or sense of duty. Someone once said: the law is far from perfect, but at the moment, it's all we've got. You will forgive me if I do not sound enthused by that notion.

Puzzled looks and dismissive shrugs were exchanged among the five. Peabody glanced to his right, where his assistant, Millie Penrith, was tapping away on a laptop, taking minutes. He'd noted sparks firing between her and one of the five, a tall, good-looking young man in his mid-to-late twenties. Peabody had a daughter only slightly younger than his pretty assistant. He could read the signs and would have a not-so-quiet word with Miss Penrith after the meeting. He'd worked so hard on this case, and the last thing he either desired or needed was her unprofessional behaviour wrecking his plans. He continued.

The envelope Mr Peabody has introduced to you contains five named files, one for each of you. Each file is for your attention and your attention only. It is vital that you do not discuss the contents with any other person. The reason for this will become obvious. Contained in each file is a request, more a plea, but one which, if acted on, will ensure that you will receive at least one-fifth share of my estate. Those present at this reading: Mr Ralph Bloomingdale, nephew. Miss Hayley Bloomingdale, niece. Mr James Wilson Patrick, cousin. Mr Wendell James Carruthers, cousin. And Mrs Connie Selznick, second cousin.

Peabody took a sip of water before drawing a letter-opener under the fold of the envelope, crunching through the wax seal. He pulled out the five buff-coloured mini-files, also sealed, and spread them out on the desk in front of him. He took a little time to compose himself before pressing on with Richard Wilkinson's instructions.

Should any of you wish to withdraw from the process at this juncture, please do so and leave with my best wishes. Your one-fifth entitlement will then be split equally among the others – as long as they carry out my wishes as expressed in their files. If all five choose to withdraw, my entire estate will go to aid cancer research, a rather obvious choice of charity which was close to my heart. Now please take a moment to make your choice.

Peabody put down his 'script', at the same time checking his watch. He clasped his bony hands together like a minister deep in prayer. Silence followed. Again, confused looks from the five.

After a full minute had elapsed, Peabody nodded towards Miss Penrith.

'The minutes will record that all five remain within the process at this juncture,' he said, once again lifting the document. 'Does anyone have any questions at this point, before we carry on to the final part of the reading?'

'I'd like to know how much we're talking about here,' James Patrick said, slightly slurring his words, his drinking-session that morning providing the required courage. 'Well, I mean, it *is* the only reason we're here, isn't it?' He leaned forward in his chair, shoulders hunched, hands held out like a pushy salesman. Ralph and Hayley Bloomingdale shook their heads. Wendell Carruthers refused to be drawn into eye-contact with the family leper. Connie Selznick sat impassively, facing the front. Finally, Patrick gave up. He shrugged at Peabody.

'Potential inheritances will be covered in more detail in due course, Mr Patrick. I would ask you to be patient. Anyone else?' Peabody said.

'Do *you* know what Uncle Richard is asking each of us to do for him?' Carruthers asked tentatively, choosing his words more carefully than his cousin.

'Since when did "that twisted old bastard" suddenly become "Uncle Richard"?' Hayley whispered in her brother's ear. He sniggered, nodding in agreement.

'I refer you to Mr Wilkinson's statement, sir,' Peabody said indignantly. 'I have absolutely no idea what is contained within each file. Each one has been sealed separately, as was the main envelope.'

'Come on, it's only a blob of wax. How easy would it be to – '

'Oh, for goodness' sake, put a sock in it, Wendell!' Connie interjected. 'The trouble with you is, you don't trust anyone. Mr Peabody is a partner in one of the most highly respected solicitors' firms in London. A million miles away from those alcoholic bar-room buddies you call every time you get caught drunk behind the wheel of that car of yours,' she added venomously.

'Sorry,' Carruthers said. He lowered his gaze, began studying his feet as if he wanted the ground to devour him, as if receiving both barrels from Connie Selznick was a regular experience for him.

'Anyone else?' Peabody asked.

'I think we should just get on with it, Mr Peabody,' Ralph said. Miss Penrith felt her pulse race, her head swim, as she listened to the handsome stranger.

'Thank you,' Peabody said, glaring at his assistant before turning his attention back to the job.

> The envelope Mr Peabody is about to open will reveal everything you are required to do to keep yourself in the running to benefit from the terms of my will. Please listen very carefully as Mr Peabody has been instructed to detail its contents once and once only.

Peabody spent a minute or so reading over the final details, then:

'Mr Wilkinson has instructed me to hand each one of you a file. As I've said, there are five, and everybody's name is handwritten on the front.' He held one up as an example. 'Miss Penrith, if you could do the honours?' Millie Penrith's gaze was again drawn to Ralph Bloomingdale as she handed him his file. More exchanged smiles, out of Peabody's line of sight. 'Oh, and yes, I have been instructed to implore you not to open the document until you have left the office.' Peabody was forced to act quickly as he watched 'mercenaries' Patrick and Carruthers fumble with theirs. 'You must study the contents and follow to the letter the guidelines set out by Mr Wilkinson. Then you will have a short time to prepare for our next meeting. This will take place one month from today, on Christmas Eve, back at this office, at exactly 2 p.m.'

'Christmas Eve? Really, Mr Peabody?' Connie asked.

'Mr Wilkinson has been quite clear on this. If people do not turn up on time for this meeting, they will be immediately excluded from the process. There will be no exceptions,' Peabody said. He turned his attention to James Patrick. 'And now, Mr Patrick, the answer to your earlier question.' Patrick and Carruthers sat forward like two fat school-kids waiting for the tuck-shop to open. 'As well as detailing any potential inheritances, I am also under instruction to explain the reason for the delay in getting to this point in the process, one full year since Mr Wilkinson's death.' As he spoke, he took time to gather up some loose papers from his desk, tucking them away neatly in a file. He placed the file inside a battered old briefcase similar to the one the Chancellor of the Exchequer might brandish on budget-day. A couple of exasperated sighs followed, with Wendell Carruthers, mindful of his proximity to Connie Selznick, careful to keep silent.

Finally, Peabody produced a folded sheet of paper from his desk diary. Opening it up, he said: 'The sale of rental properties, the realisation of unit-fund portfolios, disposal of stock, fixtures and fittings, sale of his late father's factory, the goodwill of the business, the cars ... ' He paused, as if for maximum effect. 'Most of the past year or so has been taken up by the above, all necessary to draw the estate to a conclusion. As of close of business last Friday, taking everything into consideration, and after tax, legals and miscellaneous expenses, Mr Wilkinson's net estate is valued at eight million, six hundred and eighty three thousand, four hundred and three pounds and six pence.'

Two

Ralph Bloomingdale kissed his sister Hayley goodbye before climbing into a taxi bound for his London office. Or rather, the London office where he worked. Not *his* office, you understand. Not even close. In fact, Ralph often felt as far removed from one of the firm's six senior accountants' positions as a Sunday morning hacker from Tiger Woods. Ralph worked in admin among the rest of the dreamers, peer-pressure driving them to fight and scrap like dirty dogs in the street for their one chance to impress the boss. Closing in on thirty, Ralph felt like the eternal apprentice, with a more likely prospect, especially during the current lean times, of picking up a P45 than a promotion. When Ralph had mentioned to his supervisor that he'd be late in that morning as he had been summoned to attend the reading of his uncle's will, she'd wrinkled her nose.

'Oooh, get you. Maybe you'll come back to us a millionaire,' she'd teased. He hadn't found her comments funny. Not in the slightest. Ralph hadn't two pennies to rub together, that was true, and it was no secret his uncle was loaded and as tight as the proverbial drum. Despite that, he'd always kind of liked his Uncle Richard. Granted, the old guy had had his moments. A couple of years back, he'd appeared bold as brass on the front page of a national newspaper as the man responsible for forcing the eviction of a ninety-year-old terminally-ill cancer patient and her faithful hound, Dougal, from one of his many rental properties in and around the suburbs of London. Heavy black headlines describing him as 'heartless' and 'callous', and a typically miserable-looking accompanying photograph hadn't bothered Richard Wilkinson in the slightest. During their brief lunch date at a McDonald's, Hayley and Ralph had discussed the events of the previous hour. Of course they had. To be fair, £8.5m plus change was kind of hard to ignore. When Peabody had read out the amount, there had been audible gasps in the room. Ralph and Hayley just looked at each other, resigned looks on their faces. Yes, they were technically next of kin and, by rights, should inherit most, if not all, of the old man's fortune. And yes, the terms of any inheritance seemed to hinge on whether or not some of his last wishes were carried out. But since when did Richard Wilkinson ever play things by the book? Family? Cancer organisations? No, Ralph reckoned the smart money was on the arts. Opera would be a good bet, he mused; and not because Uncle Richard loved opera. Far from it: he absolutely loathed it. But maybe if he thought he could encourage the growth of this torture by investing his millions in it, he'd do it in a heartbeat. Perhaps his warped mind had it worked out that the silver-spoon brigade went to opera only because they maintained it was the right thing to do for people of fine breeding. That secretly they hated the yowling as much as he did. Yes, opera ... or maybe bagpipe manufacturers. 'Twenty-five cats fighting inside a tartan sack,' he'd often sneer.

'And this business with Christmas,' Ralph said. 'You know the reason for that, don't you?'

'Have a great Christmas,' Hayley replied in her best Uncle Richard voice. 'Oh, and by the way, I'm giving you bugger-all!'

'Something like.'

Ralph and Hayley had been first on the scene when their uncle had taken ill, only because they were used to visiting him regularly. After Wilkinson's lackeys located the other three, at least two had swept into town with the rumble of the gravy-train far outweighing the downside of actually having to spend some time with the old man. As it transpired, the trio barely had time to be re-united with their long-lost cousin before he was taken by acute cancer of the pancreas. At twenty-seven, a year younger than her brother, Hayley Bloomingdale fully expected to be celebrating her next birthday still setting, blow-drying, curling and perming hair in the claustrophobic cupboard she called 'Hayley's Boutique': the place where she would often allow her mind to drift away during a blue rinse; the place where she'd break into fits of giggles when recalling one piece of sound advice from her brother: 'Be careful when you put your key in the lock. You might break the window!' At the end of the day, Hayley poked what was left of a chicken curry takeaway around her plate. Sitting on her tiny couch, watching her tiny TV in the tiny living room of her tiny flat above her tiny boutique, she sighed deeply and began to imagine a changed life: a bigger life, yes, of course, but a different kind of life; a life where she would be free to go anywhere she liked, any time she liked and with whom she liked; a life where she would never again need to rob Peter, or compromise on quality, or settle for second best. She glanced firstly at her watch, then at the buff file sitting in the centre of the coffee-table beside her. Her breathing quickened. She felt woozy. Her heart fluttered. *What if?*

It was almost 8 p.m., the time the brother and sister had agreed on at lunch. She counted down the last ten seconds, as if she were about to launch a rocket from Cape Kennedy. On the count of 'one', she had the file on her lap, sliding a slender finger along it. She drew in a long breath as she eased out the contents and began to read. Five minutes later, a shocked Hayley Bloomingdale quietly laid the information back down on the coffee-table just as her brother's name and face flashed up in her mobile display. She could only watch as the phone buzzed across the table, eventually coming to rest perched right on the edge. Ralph tried again after a few seconds, the first vibration toppling the phone on to the floor.

She reached down to switch it off.

Three

Hayley hadn't slept well. Sod's Law. She'd seen every hour on the clock and, now that it was 7.30 a.m. and almost time for her to get ready to open the shop, she realised she was going to have a fight on her hands to stay awake. She'd expected Ralph to appear at her door in the middle of the night, especially since she'd kept her mobile switched off. He hadn't. She switched the phone on, hit the number for her message box. 'You have no new messages,' the voice droned in her ear. Her mind raced into overdrive: he really is going to do it! Uncle Richard, via the file, had stressed that there was to be no contact among the five. Crikey, what if he really is ... She threw the duvet to one side and swung her legs off the bed, pausing for a moment to let her senses catch up. Washing her hands over her face, she gulped in deep breaths as huge shivers coursed up and down her body. She began to cry. Then crying gave way to nausea, and soon Hayley was racing into the toilet and vomiting down the pan. Afterwards, she stumbled into her kitchen, so tiny it really was a kind of mini-kitchenette, if one could imagine such a thing. Holding a piece of tissue-paper against her mouth in case she felt like throwing up again, she flicked the kettle-switch, shovelled coffee and sugar into a mug and walked through to her tiny lounge.

Hayley glanced at her watch as she nestled down into her favourite chair, pulling the straps of her nightdress over her bare shoulders. 7.45 a.m. Her gaze was drawn to the coffee-table and the file and its contents, still sprawled out on top. Her next instinct was to feed everything into the shredder and forget about the whole thing. Next-door, the kettle bubbled and groaned before clicking off. She checked her watch again. 7.49 a.m. She considered pouring the coffee, making some toast, but the mere thought brought another wave of nausea. Luckily, she wasn't really a breakfast person anyway. Her clothes for that day were sitting beside her, neatly folded. Some more minutes passed. Another glance at her watch. 7.56 a.m. I have to move! The shop won't open itself! I have appointments! Oh, what do I do? She walked back through to her tiny kitchen, stopping to rip a piece of paper from a notepad stuck to the back of the door. Fumbling in her cutlery drawer, she produced a black permanent marker-pen and a roll of sellotape. She wrote:

HAYLEY'S BOUTIQUE CLOSED TODAY (25th NOVEMBER) OWING TO ILLNESS. APOLOGIES FOR ANY INCONVENIENCE CAUSED. PLEASE RE-BOOK FOR SPECIAL HALF-PRICE OFFER.

Hayley Bloomingdale (Proprietor).

Three minutes later, the sign taped to the inside of her shop window, Hayley was on her way back to the flat. She was almost at the top of her stairs when she heard her mobile ring. Her heart bumped in a couple of double beats when she saw the name of her brother light up in the display. This time she *was* ready to talk to him.

Four

Two weeks later. Kevin Laxdale was a creature of habit. He rose at the same time every morning, showered and dressed. He sat at his breakfast-table in a neatly ironed white shirt and blue silk tie, black slacks and black suede loafers, chewing away at his lightly-browned toast. He waited for the Radio 2 pips signifying 8 a.m., snatched his car-keys from the worktop and headed into town.

As always he took the long route, swinging past a small primary school on the edge of town, slowing to allow the lollipop-lady to step out on to the crossing and guide the children across the road. Laxdale smiled and waved at a couple of boys a few steps behind the rest. The boys smiled and waved back, which really made his day. Ten minutes later, Laxdale was taking the steps up to the library.

"Morning, Karen,' he said as he breezed through the door. Karen Witherspoon, chief librarian, did not respond but visibly stiffened as her assistant brushed past. Just as she visibly stiffened every single day she'd clapped eyes on him since the court case: same feeling, different day. For the past five years, Karen had spent the majority of her working life praying for Kevin Laxdale's holidays to come round. And every time they did, she'd torture herself with guilt as she imagined some of the despicable horrors he might unleash on some unsuspecting child. She felt physically sick each time she recalled the day Laxdale first walked into her life. The handsome, fresh-faced twenty three-year-old stirred something inside the attractive divorcee, even at his initial interview. Twelve years older, she'd been seduced by his good looks, his wit, manner, charm. The whole package had blown the other candidates away. There could be only one possible choice. After his appointment, unable - or unwilling - to resist his charms, Karen had dated Laxdale a couple of times. Mercifully, the only thing she had shared with him was a bucket of popcorn at the local cinema. On the morning of their third date, Laxdale hadn't appeared for work. Karen had known right off something was wrong. Laxdale was never late for anything, especially work. She hadn't known him for long but had already identified a couple of idiosyncrasies. Nothing sinister, she recalled thinking, in wanting to be somewhere on time or trying to avoid stepping on the lines on a pavement.

As events unfolded during the day of his arrest, another of Kevin Laxdale's more serious penchants was to hit the headlines. Two boys, aged twelve and ten, had been attacked in separate incidents at local parks a few weeks previously. The method and intensity of the sadistic rape, beatings and torture displayed during the second assault was such that the police were able to link it straight away with the first attack. Police forensics had further cemented that link via traces of saliva and semen from both crime scenes. Then the authorities reached stalemate having trawled various databases in the hope of finding a DNA match. Kevin Laxdale was finally fingered for the crimes after some vigilante reporter on one of the local rags managed to drum up enough public support to empower every male in the town to attend the community hall to provide a cheek-swab. A week later, a story involving one of the detectives working on the case hit the hopes for a conviction stone dead when it was reported he had used 'force greater than necessary' when arresting Kevin Laxdale. Turned out the detective had been the first victim's uncle and, yes, he had gone to town on Laxdale. Then another cock-up, this time a technical breach by some dozy idiot in the admin department, meant that the case was unlikely even to reach an initial hearing. The determination of an under-pressure police department, allied to the considerable sway of public opinion, did indeed manage to get Kevin Laxdale as far as Judge Richard Wilkinson's courtroom.

The judge spent little time reading the case-history before proceeding to wipe the floor with everybody: the police for their 'monumental lack of professionalism and crass stupidity', the media for 'whipping the community into a frenzy on the back of a case that Kevin Laxdale's defence lawyer could drive a bus through'. And Laxdale himself, whom Wilkinson described as 'conniving, evil and gutless'. In the end, Judge Richard Wilkinson found himself with no option but to throw out the case for the prosecution. Laxdale had smiled from ear to ear, even winked at the judge as he delivered the news. Wilkinson would later admit to colleagues that, just at that precise moment, he'd have happily killed Kevin Laxdale, there and then, slap-bang in the middle of his courtroom.

In a sad postscript, as well as the detective who committed the assault on Laxdale losing his job, pension and all, the second victim was unable to cope with what had happened to him, and, three years later, decided to take his own life. Incredibly, Kevin

Laxdale had managed to hang on to his job. A cash-strapped council, rather than having to deal with an employment-tribunal, where, no doubt, the 'unfortunate' individual would be portrayed as 'innocent' and 'a victim', decided to do absolutely nothing. 'As soon as he steps out of line, we'll have him. His feet won't touch the ground,' her head of department had promised a horrified Karen Witherspoon. Five years later, Laxdale still hadn't put a foot wrong. He'd been the model employee. Nevertheless, Karen lived in hope. She continued to bide her time. Her mind was made up: if she saw Kevin Laxdale as much as sneeze the wrong way, it would be the end of the road for him.

5.00 p.m.: Laxdale's car slipped in alongside the rush-hour traffic heading for the outskirts of town. It was Monday, and his normal itinerary for that day would detail a light dinner at his usual table for one in the corner of Lex's Bistro, the restaurant part of Micklewhite's Hotel, followed by a twenty-minute dip in the leisure-centre's pool. And, if he timed it right, as he invariably did, he might hit the changing-room at the same time as the Sinclairs and the Harveys, two families that also used the facility on a regular basis. Laxdale had done his best to charm his way into their circle. At the moment it was barely more than a nod to both parents. Of course, it wasn't the parents who interested or excited him. It was the four young boys they brought with them. Laxdale estimated their ages at somewhere between nine and thirteen. After all, he did have some experience on the subject. So much so, he'd lie awake at night fantasising about their slim, white bodies brushing against his in the pool.

Both families were in the changing-area as Laxdale walked in. Each time he'd do his best to choose a locker close to them, but not too close. The last thing he wanted was to undo all the hard work it had taken to get to that point with a stray glance in the wrong direction. Laxdale nodded at both fathers as he walked past, heading for the locker nearest the door to the poolside. The boys, completely oblivious to the predator in their midst, ran past Laxdale, the lad at the front stopping to grab the door's metal handle. Laxdale smiled at him as he reached above his head for the handle, easing the door open. All four excitedly filed past. Just before the door sucked shut, Laxdale heard the sound of their bodies hitting the water. His heart drummed loudly in his chest. Three minutes later, a towel over his arm and a book in his hand, Laxdale was making his way over to a small table set next to a bubbling jacuzzi. As he sat at the table, laying the book and towel down on the chair next to him, he took the opportunity to take a look around: there were seven other people in the pool-area that night – probably about average for a Monday. The Taylors and the Harveys made four, a young couple in the jacuzzi made six, and another man sitting on the edge of the pool, his feet dangling in the water, completed the set.

Laxdale had never seen the man before. He estimated him to be around fifty. He was overweight, with curly red hair and an even redder face. Although the man, to Laxdale, didn't look much like a policeman, he couldn't afford to take a chance. He just couldn't. One slip, that's all it would take. Bide your time, Kevin. There's always tomorrow. Laxdale was feeling chuffed to bits that he'd stayed in his chair while the boys cavorted in front of him. Outwardly, he remained calm, but inside, as ever, he was battling the urges. Half-an-hour had passed, and everyone had exited the pool area, except Kevin Laxdale and the stranger. The man had been swimming slowly, back and forth across the pool for the past five minutes or so. Laxdale decided to join him and try and get rid of some of his frustration with a few quick lengths. He put down the paperback, stood and plunged in. Halfway across length four, he felt a stinging pain in his leg. The drug took effect almost immediately. Laxdale tried to scream but could not make a sound. Very quickly, muscles all over his body went into spasm and, although he was within touching distance of the edge of the pool, he was unable to reach for it. The pool attendant was visible through a slim window set in the door to reception. Please, oh, please turn around. Why can't you hear me? Laxdale was certain he was screaming at the man. He was sure he could hear his voice loud and strong, reverberating around the tiny pool area as he slipped under for the last time. That night, death came particularly slowly and painfully for Kevin Laxdale. And it came exactly as Richard Wilkinson had planned it.

Wendell Carruthers, legs like soft rubber, was back in his car heading down the tight drive of the hotel when the ambulance screamed past him. His heart lurched as the realisation of what he had just done hit home. 'The syringe!' he cried, fumbling in his jacket pocket. He exhaled slowly with relief when he eventually found it in the opposite pocket. Carruthers had possessed the presence of mind to slip the safety-cover on the syringe before he even reached the changing room. After that, things became a little hazy. Now that the deed was done, he was in no doubt as to his next course of action. Over the last couple of weeks, he'd replayed this moment in his mind a hundred times. Once on the main road, Carruthers pulled over into the first lay-by he came to and hit speed-dial on his mobile phone. A robot voice cut in on the second ring and guided him through some menu options. As Richard Wilkinson had promised, he'd then received a personal six-digit code which he scribbled down excitedly. All he had to do now was look forward to a profitable Christmas.

Five

Christmas Eve. Miss Penrith and Mr Percy Harwood of Peabody, Stoughton and Harwood were the only two people in the firm's boardroom. In fact, apart from a token security-guard, they were the only two people in the building, given the date. Miss Penrith sat poised, laptop open for business. She chewed nervously at her nails as she waited. Harwood glanced at the clock on the wall: 1.55 p.m. He'd had to react quickly after he received an unexpected telephone-call only one hour before from Mr Peabody, informing him that he would have to 'deal with the Wilkinson case' following Peabody's 'family emergency.' Harwood lived only five minutes' drive from the office, so it had been no problem for him then to call Miss Penrith in order that she could make her way in earlier than planned and have the official minutes of the first meeting on his desk before the beneficiaries arrived. He could then familiarise himself with the case. It made good business sense – no surprises.

Harwood's wife's parents always landed on his doorstep on Christmas Eve. It had become, for him at least, an unwanted family tradition, a kind of unpleasant 'dry run' leading up to the main event. His tricky exercise for the day was working out a raft of apologies for his wife, children and in-laws. Someone else would have to deck the halls and carve the turkey. The Wilkinson case was worth far too much money to the firm to worry about hurting some yuletide feelings. Harwood slid the aforementioned minutes to one side when he heard the front office-door creaking open, footsteps drawing closer. Ralph and Hayley Bloomingdale and Wendell Carruthers filed in and took their seats at the other side of the table. Ralph smiled at Millie Penrith as he made himself comfortable. She glanced to her left towards Percy Harwood, who was too busy writing notes on a pad to notice. Her immediate boss, Mr Peabody, had 'marked her cards' in no uncertain manner, following her 'brazenly flirtatious behaviour' (his words) during the first meeting. Coast clear, she smiled back. Wendell Carruthers looked even redder than normal, as if his face was ready to explode. Ralph had detected a trace of disappointment in Carruthers' face when the three of them arrived outside for the meeting.

'Wendell obviously thought he'd be the only one to turn up,' Ralph had whispered to his sister. 'He wasn't banking on having to split the money three ways.' By the look on his face, Carruthers had obviously got over his disappointment; no doubt with the aid of some more simple arithmetic. The whole lot would have been great, but, all going well, soon Wendell would be sliding his stubby fingers through more than two and a half million quid! Given his current, dead-end-job and gloomy prospects, it would do just fine.

'Merry Christmas, everyone,' Harwood said cheerily enough. 'Thank you for coming. First up, I must make apologies for Mr Peabody who, unfortunately could not - ' He was interrupted by the door to the boardroom flying open and three men rushing in. Two of the men were dressed in police uniform, the third in plain clothes – cream raincoat, suit, shirt and tie. The plain-clothed policeman, a tall man in his late forties, scanned the faces around the table until his gaze landed on the panic-stricken face of Wendell Carruthers.

'Forgive the interruption,' he said, deadpan, not averting his gaze from Carruthers. 'Everybody please remain seated.'

'What is going on here? This is a private meeting,' Harwood said, indignantly.

'And you are?' the policeman asked, switching his attention to the lawyer.

'Percy Harwood. I'm one of the partners of the firm.'

'Detective Inspector Miller of the Metropolitan Police Force. And this is Constable Lewis and Constable Fraser.' Lewis stood by Wendell Carruthers' left shoulder and Fraser covered the door as Miller walked round behind Harwood to face the three beneficiaries. Carruthers' face was now chalk-white.

'I think you've come to the wrong place, inspector,' Harwood said.

'Then maybe you can explain this, Mr Harwood.' Miller reached into his coat-pocket and pulled out an envelope which he handed to Harwood. Harwood looked at the envelope for a few seconds. An hour and a half previously he was getting ready to tuck into Christmas turkey with all the trimmings. Now what? Huffing out a sigh, he slipped the letter from the envelope, propped up his glasses and began to read. About half-way through, Harwood glanced briefly at Wendell Carruthers before returning his attention to the document. Carruthers had heard enough. He slid his chair back, ducking under Lewis' grasp and bolted for the door. Fraser spun him round and pinned him to the floor, face down, before forcing both wrists behind his back. Lewis 'cuffed him. Then both he and Fraser hauled him to his feet.

'Read him his rights and get him out of here,' Inspector Miller commanded. 'I'll meet you back at the station later.'

'Right, sir,' Lewis said, pulling on the chain-link between the 'cuffs. Fraser began the reading of rights as all three left the room. Percy Harwood wasn't often lost for words. This was one of those rare moments. He placed the letter down on the table, unsure of how he should proceed.

'May I?' Miller asked. Harwood didn't answer at first, eventually nodding as he emerged from a kind of confused trance. Miller began to pace around the table.

'The letter sitting in front of Mr Harwood,' he went on, 'was hand-delivered to New Scotland Yard at precisely twelve o'clock today, as per the writer's instructions. It was handed in by a staff-member of the firm of lawyers, Hudson and Harman. It appears the letter had been held in the firm's time-vault for the past twelve months. It is addressed "strictly private and confidential" and for my personal attention and bears the seal of the late Judge Richard Wilkinson.' He walked over to the door and pressed the button in the middle of the door-knob, locking them in. 'Ordinarily, it would be remiss of me to discuss the finer details relating to any murder-investigation, but in this case I am willing to make an exception.' He pulled back the now-vacant chair and sat at Ralph and Hayley's right-hand side. He continued: 'You see, my policeman's instincts tell me there's a lot more to this matter than meets the eye.'

'Please enlighten us, inspector,' a resigned Percy Harwood said, as he leaned back in his chair, folding his arms.

'About two weeks ago, unconfirmed child-rapist, Kevin Laxdale, was found drowned in the pool at his local hotel's leisure-centre.'

'Yes, I read the report in the newspaper. It said the police suspected a heart-attack or stroke,' Hayley said, before adding: 'Sorry, I'm Hayley Bloomingdale, Richard Wilkinson's niece, and this is my brother, Ralph.' Miller nodded at both.

'Yes, we did suspect a dodgy ticker, at first,' he said.

'But the papers didn't mention anything about his being a child-rapist, inspector,' Hayley continued.

'That's because technically he's not, but the evidence we had against him was overwhelming. The scumbag got off on a technicality. And the judge who was forced to throw out the case was - '

'Uncle Richard,' Hayley finished the sentence.

'That's right.'

'But what has his death to do with any of this?' Hayley asked.

'As you'll have gathered, Laxdale didn't die of a heart-attack or a stroke. The pathologist found an unusually high dosage of succinylcholine in his blood stream. Without getting too technical, it's a neuro-muscular blocking drug that can quickly cause paralysis of vocal chords, relaxation of muscles, that type of thing. It can paralyse the muscles needed to breathe.'

'So he drowned because of this drug?' Hayley asked.

'Undoubtedly. On closer inspection our pathologist found the needle-mark in Laxdale's right leg. '

'And Wendell - ?'

'That's right. Judge Wilkinson's letter names Laxdale as the victim and Wendell Carruthers as his killer, along with exactly how he did it.'

'B-but how is this possible? You said this letter has been in a time-vault for the past year,' Harwood said.

'That's where I need a little help filling in the blanks.' Miller's gaze swept across the four faces in the room.

'Maybe I can help with that, inspector,' Ralph said. Miller, like the good policeman he was, looked into Ralph's eyes as if he were looking deep into his very soul, searching for signs of character.

'All right, Mr Bloomingdale, you have my attention,' he said. Ralph reached down to the floor and pulled a pile of letters and files from a satchel at his feet. He arranged them neatly in front of him. Glancing at his sister, as if for reassurance, he began.

'One month ago, Hayley and I, along with Wendell Carruthers, James Patrick and Connie Selznick attended a meeting pre-arranged by my late uncle, Richard Wilkinson, at this office. The firm's Mr Peabody chaired the meeting and Miss Penrith kindly took the minutes.' Smiles exchanged between them. 'Towards the end, Mr Peabody handed each one of us a file which he said contained details of a request we had to complete for Uncle Richard before this meeting today.'

'What kind of request?' Miller asked.

'I'll cover that in a minute, inspector. Basically, whoever did not do as Uncle Richard had asked, no matter the reason, would not be eligible for any portion of his inheritance.'

'Which explains why the other two aren't here now?' Miller said.

'Yes.'

'And you have no idea what they had been asked to do, Mr Bloomingdale?'

'As a matter of fact, I have, inspector,' Ralph said. 'I believe the requests that Connie and James received were similar to the ones my uncle asked of me and Hayley.'

'Which were?' Ralph shifted a little uncomfortably, glancing nervously at his sister. 'Mr Bloomingdale?' Miller asked again.

'He asked us to, in his words, "perform an invaluable public service by helping to rid society of its blood-sucking, predatory scum".'

'To commit murder?' Miller asked.

'Yes.'

'Which is why we have just arrested Wendell Carruthers.' Ralph nodded. Miller laid both hands on the table, leaning down to make eye-contact with Ralph. 'Then by your and your sister's attendance here today, I assume both of you have confessions to make?' Percy Harwood's jaw almost hit his knees at the revelation. He stared blankly at Ralph.

'I can assure you, inspector, Hayley, Connie, James and I haven't killed anyone,' Ralph said. Miller thought for a moment.

'The floor's still yours, Mr Bloomingdale,' he said.

'Thank you. The day after the first meeting, I received an envelope from the same firm of solicitors you mentioned earlier, Hudson and Harman. Inside was another letter from Uncle Richard, apologising for causing unavoidable stress and discomfort via his first instruction. He advised me to ignore the first letter and sit tight until the morning of the Christmas Eve meeting, when all would be revealed.'

'And just whom did his first letter ask you to kill?'

'Nobody, as it turned out.'

'Don't mess with me, Mr Bloomingdale!' Miller snapped. 'I'm of a mind to haul everybody down to the station to continue with this.'

'Sorry, inspector. What I meant to say was that the name of the person I was asked to kill was fictitious. He didn't exist.'

'But why go through with the charade?'

'It was for someone else's benefit. Don't worry, Inspector. I'll get to that in a minute.'

'And your sister and the others?' Miller took off his coat, laying it neatly on the back of a chair. He loosened his tie as he spoke.

'The same. When I received Uncle Richard's second letter, I called Hayley right away. I'm glad I did. She was pretty shaken up after the first letter.' He patted the back of her hand. 'Hayley also received her letter from Hudson and Harman later that day, with, more or less, the same explanation.'

'And the others?' Miller asked.

'I spoke with Connie first. She blabbed something about Uncle Richard being a "silly old sod" and that she didn't need his money anyway. Then she hung up. James Patrick sounded drunk when I spoke to him. I couldn't get a whole lot of sense. Something about him "not getting a thin dime as he'd only blow it on the booze".' Ralph chuckled.

'And Carruthers?' Miller asked, ignoring this unsavoury side-light on a member of the family.

Ralph shrugged. 'Couldn't get hold of him. I assumed he'd received the same second letter. Obviously I was wrong.'

'So only Carruthers' man was real?' Miller said, scratching the stubble on his chin. And the judge's plan was for Kevin Laxdale to die. But then why turn Carruthers in afterwards? I know we'd figured out how Laxdale was killed, but it would have taken a huge slice of luck to actually collar Carruthers.'

'Uncle Richard hated Wendell. And his father. Wendell was arrested a few years back on charges of molesting a young boy. Hayley and I were very young when it happened, but I remember stories of Wendell's father lying for him. The charges were dropped in the end.'

'And the old man must've known Carruthers would do what he asked. Stitched him up like a kipper.' Miller smiled ruefully.

'I guess so.'

'But then why go through the sham of sending the other four letters? Why not leave it at Carruthers, especially as the rest were fictitious?'

'The answer's in here, inspector. It was handed in this morning, just after nine. Same lawyers, same instructions. Uncle Richard mentions you by name, says you were one of the few policemen he could trust and that I should pass this on to you.' Ralph selected another envelope with remnants of the same broken wax seal on the back and pushed it across the polished table for the policeman. 'Uncle Richard says "Merry Christmas",' Ralph added, smiling. DI Miller stared at the envelope for a few seconds. He was probably dreading the paperwork this latest letter would provoke. He had known Judge Wilkinson. Their paths had crossed in court on a couple of occasions, and, although he had never received an easy ride when in front of him, Miller respected the old man's integrity. It had obviously been a two-way thing. Miller slipped the letter from the envelope, spread it out flat in front of him. His eyes widened, and his brow furrowed, as he read. Finally, he folded the letter and put it neatly back in the envelope. He turned to Percy Harwood and asked:

'Where's Fred Peabody?'

'He called me earlier. Said there had been some kind of family emergency. You see, technically, this is his case. But why? I don't understand. Has Fred done something wrong, inspector?' Harwood stood to face Miller.

'I'd sit down if I were you,' Miller said. Harwood glanced at Ralph Bloomingdale, who nodded in agreement. Miller continued: 'The reason Judge Wilkinson's original instructions to the five beneficiaries were lodged with Peabody, Stoughton and Harwood was simple. It was a piece of an elaborate jigsaw, a plan to ensnare someone. And it worked.' Miller watched the expression on Harwood's face change to a bright shade of mystified pink. He couldn't be absolutely sure, but he would have staked his police pension on Percy Harwood having played no part in the deception. 'Judge Wilkinson engineered the whole thing.' Miller stood and began to prowl the room, like a lion dividing a herd of antelope, cutting out the weak. 'He sent letters to all five, knowing full well Peabody would have his nose stuck right into them. Peabody was easily convinced that the judge had set up offshore accounts for the five, complete with a code which each would receive after he or she had completed the task he had set. On

Christmas Eve - today – each person in attendance would be asked to punch in his or her code. Then, in a few seconds, their share of the cash, activated by their personal code, would be electronically transferred to their designated account.'

'Good Lord!' Harwood cried. 'He's stolen that money, hasn't he? This is terrible! We're finished!' His hands shook uncontrollably as he tried to pour himself a glass of water. Miss Penrith leaned across and took over, setting the glass down in front of her boss. He nodded his thanks as he sipped the water.

'No, but he would probably have got away with it, Mr Harwood, if it hadn't been for a certain member of your staff,' Miller said.

'What do you mean?' Harwood asked.

'All of Judge Wilkinson's money has been re-routed into one account at the bank, sir.' Millie Penrith said. 'Just as Mr Peabody had planned.'

'But h-how?'

'I had a word with the bank-manager there - Mr Russell. He was extremely helpful,' she added, smiling.

'I don't understand,' Harwood admitted.

'Last year, I also received an interesting letter from Judge Wilkinson. The letter highlighted a string of legal cases from some years back. All of these cases involved estate-succession and alleged fraud and deception, where sums of money appeared to vanish mysteriously without trace. And all of them involved Mr Peabody. While senior partner in another law-firm, he'd been asked to act on behalf of the family of a recently-deceased widow, a Mrs Gloria Tompkins. To cut a long story short, in what should have been a straight-forward winding up and disposal of her estate, a total of around £40,000 went missing. Investigations turned up nothing. Legally, there was nothing that could be done.'

'I had no idea,' Harwood said. 'But why did Judge Wilkinson contact you, Miss Penrith?'

'The judge knew I would do everything in my power to help, sir, because Gloria Tompkins was my grandmother. And Bill Russell, the manager at the bank, is my step-father.' Percy

Harwood thanked his assistant. He smiled, probably at the relief of knowing his clients' funds were safe.

'So what happens now, inspector?' he asked.

'I'd better put a call in to the station,' Miller replied.

'That won't be necessary, inspector,' Millie said.

'But what about Fred Peabody?' Harwood asked.

'Technically, we don't have enough to convict him right now,' Miller said. 'He could easily say he's keeping the funds safe in a company-account, gathering interest, until the inheritances are announced. No, we need to wait until he tries to withdraw the money. I'd like to know what Miss Penrith has in mind, though.'

'I'm hoping the police are already involved by now, inspector,' Millie said.

'When will we know?' Harwood asked.

'When my step-father calls my mobile.' As if choreographed, the mobile phone burst into life. A quick exchange before Millie said:

'The police have arrested him,' as she flicked the screen to end the call. 'Bill said Mr Peabody turned up at the bank an hour ago. He managed to stall him while he got a member of staff to call the police. They caught him red-handed with passport in his pocket and suitcase in his car, getting ready to do a runner.'

'Fantastic!' Ralph said, flashing a huge smile at Millie Penrith. He was looking forward to their Boxing Day dinner-date.

'So it's over,' Hayley Bloomingdale commented.

'Not quite,' said Ralph, pulling another document from his proverbial hat. 'This also came earlier today. It's addressed to Stoughton and Harwood. Mr Harwood, could you do the honours?' Ralph handed the plain brown envelope to the lawyer. Once again, the envelope bore the same red wax seal as before. Harwood freed the letter. He scanned the document quickly, a puzzled look crossing his face when he reached the end.

'Mr Harwood?' Ralph said. Harwood placed the letter on the table. 'It's Judge Wilkinson's last will and testament, revoking the earlier arrangements. It looks to be perfectly acceptable. He apologises to the remaining partners of my firm and details a deserved bonus to be paid to us from the estate, but - '

'But what?' Hayley asked.

'The judge appears to have left everything to some amateur opera company in the West End!' Ralph and Hayley Bloomingdale burst out laughing.

'Nettlewoods'
Steve Morris

I tried to find the address without my glasses.

'Why on earth do councils hide street signs?' I fumed. Having finally given up driving in circles around streets that all looked the same this time of year, I parked the car in frustration and continued the rest of the way on foot. I squinted at each house doorway as I pulled up my coat collar to keep the wind from the back of my neck. There was never anywhere to park any more, even if you did arrive in a police car. I didn't mind being at work over Christmas: I just didn't like to be out in the cold, especially with the cough I'd developed that week. 'It's no help that people put names instead of numbers on their doors now,' I remember grumbling. '"Nettlewoods"? What's the point of house names in a street of a hundred houses?' I really was only pretending to be angry that night. More likely all this was more to do with resenting having to leave a nice warm office. The fact that I was relaxed enough to think about something other than a messy corpse in a murder scene in front of me was a sign, if ever there was one, that I had been doing the job for far too long.

The streets that evening were understandably very quiet around the suburb. The only place showing busy activity was the Foresters' Arms, although I didn't wish I were in there instead. Scotch in my desk drawer would do for me instead of all this Merry Christmas stuff later that night. Many houses looked the same - as did each street, for that matter. Multi-coloured fairy lights were visible in most windows, and the incandescent flicker of television screens was the only sign of life visible behind thinner curtains. It *was* a textbook Christmas Eve after all, complete with frost and a clear sky. Some of these decorations had probably been up for months. Silly season seemed to start earlier every year.

'Christmas starts for me in September too, unfortunately,' I thought to myself as I squinted under a street-lamp and tilted the note paper to read the address I'd been given at the station by the desk sergeant. Or in other words: 'I start hating Christmas the moment shops start putting pressure on everyone to enjoy something that some of us will always dread.' Judging by the writing on the note, the desk sergeant had been on the pop early, too. He had Christmas Day off. 'I'm responsible for enforcing the law, and there's no law to say that you have to celebrate Christmas,' I decided as I crossed the road. Then with the annual small lump in my throat, I realised that I deliberately allowed myself to draw the short straw every festive season and go to work because I had nothing at home worth doing or celebrating all that week. Working was a good excuse to avoid the festive period altogether. Of course, each December I'd make out how hard-done-by I was, but in reality duty gave me something worth getting up for on Christmas morning and distracted me from my domestic emptiness. People *needed* a police detective sergeant even at this time of year. What they *didn't need* was a spare regretful mid-fifties guy pretending to make merry in the absence of any surviving relatives. New Year was another problem for me, but then most of us would be on duty anyway this year. We would see what fun and games 1980 would bring us. It was amazing how busy Christmas can be for the murder-squad every year. Perhaps it was because many families were forced to spend time together, confined indoors in the warmth, when everything outside was cold and closed down.

By the time I found the address, 'Nettlewoods' already had two squad cars parked (badly) on the road outside it. The husband, a Mr Nettles, had been found dead by his wife a few hours before, with his throat slit wide open. 'They had better not have bumped any residents' cars again,' I thought. Mr Nettles was retired and in his early 60s, but that was all I knew so far. There was nothing on file about him back at the station. I fastened the top button on my coat after another coughing fit before I entered the house. 'So much for goodwill to all men. Compliments of the season.'

One constable stood by the front door of the Edwardian terrace that (judging by the slightly rotting cream sash window frames), had seen much better days. Curtains and nets twitched from every angle on both sides of the road. *'Neighbours would miss Morecambe and Wise tonight. At least viewers were warm inside. It is time to forget Christmas and roll my sleeves up.'* That suited me.

'He's in there, sarge,' the first said, nodding me towards a side door to the left of the hallway. 'Where's your car?' I nodded back down the street without saying anything else. I knew I'd end up with these two together. They were well-known back at the station for being especially lazy, but for once I sympathised with them to some extent. It *was* Christmas Eve, after all, and, unlike me, they probably had better things to do. But then I also remembered they were earning double time. As I passed between them, I was sure I smelled Scotch on the breath of at least one. You can't go out and buy a sense of smell like mine. That had come in handy a few times over the years.

'Put your fags out. Show some respect,' I said, long after I'd walked past them. They both knew what I meant.

The inside of the house was pleasantly warm, almost making up for the mess under the sheet.

'Go on,' I told the WPC who was in the room with the body.

'The doc had to give Mrs Nettles a sedative. She was in quite a state, sarge. Came downstairs to find him like this,' she told me, before she got out her notebook and went on to summarise what she had found when she arrived at the scene. Those two outside had a lot to learn from her.

'Blast. I've left my glasses on my desk *again*,' I moaned, as I held my hand out at arm's length and pretended I couldn't read the handwriting. 'I think it says on this paper that his missus found this Edward Nettles with his throat cut after she'd been upstairs.' I had a close look at the body as best I could without my specs. Despite the mess, he was almost peaceful, as if he had been caught completely unawares. The surgery had been done quickly and, by the looks of it, by someone who knew what they were doing. I could have done with another good cough, but it didn't seem the proper time and place. 'This is admittedly quite brutal,' I thought.

'Why had this happened and who'd done it? Significantly though, why tonight? Pre-meditated murderers have better things to do on Christmas Eve.'

'Did you ask the neighbours,' I asked out loud, 'whether they'd heard any quarrelling lately?' WPC French knew what I was thinking. She wasn't sloppy, like the two lads outside. I hoped that the cold would sober them up.

'No. Nothing, sarge.'

'Do you think … ?' I nodded upstairs.

'No, sarge. She's in no fit state.'

'She might have been up to it a few hours ago, though. Now she's probably realising what she's done,' I said, before going back to look again more closely at the body. WPC French went on:

'Mrs Nettles says she was in the bath. She heard a commotion downstairs and came down and found him like this. Thought he was watching telly. No sign of anyone. Doors were unlocked.' I still suspected the spouse. It was often the case.

'Did you check the bathroom?'

'Yes, someone did have a bath at that time.'

'*His* razor?'

'No, he uses one of those new electric things.'

'They're no good. They never get anything like close enough. I hope you didn't get me one for Christmas. I'll ask her what film he was watching. Next of kin? Relatives?'

'No. None apparently on either side.'

'No one? Really? I thought only I was that negligent.'

Another man in a long coat and big black glasses came in through the front door to add another cold draught from outside. *'Will you close that flaming door? Do these people never feel the cold? Was he born in a barn?'*

'Compliments of the season, sarge,' the latest figure said sarcastically. The police photographer had arrived. I didn't bother to look at him to see whether he was smiling or frowning. Neither did I bother to return his compliment. He knew I hated the season.

He was a regular presence when investigations were about three hours old, and it was only when I saw him begin twisting and snapping that I noticed from the expression on his face he was someone else who clearly resented being dragged out of the pub on Christmas Eve.

Five minutes later there was more activity outside. One of the bobbies seemed to be spending the evening continually opening and closing the front door to give us a running commentary on who was arriving. Perhaps he wanted us to feel how cold it was out there. 'Helpful' neighbours were being turned away from the gates, and then the first of the press photographers began to lurk outside on the street. It was certainly getting colder out there.

'Oh, let 'em freeze! They'll soon get bored out there tonight,' I told the two constables. 'I want fingerprints taken now on the doors, including the interior ones.'

At that point, I realised that it was time for me to take a closer look around the property before the whole place got trampled. I liked to get a feel of the crime scene.

The large sitting room at 'Nettlewoods' was comfortable enough for anyone, without being luxurious by any means. I could easily have sunk into Mr Nettles' armchair and into his life. The room still felt warm and stuffy from the gas-fire that might have been on all that day. If it hadn't have been so damned cold outside, I'd have been tempted to lift a sash window before I noticed that they had all been taped around the edges to prevent draughts. This had been done the previous winter, to judge from how yellow the tape had gone.

Modest streamers, some having repaired tears in them from several previous Decembers, had been twisted and taped to hang between the walls and from the dominant cold bright 100-watt dusty ceiling pendant light over the centre of the Artex ceiling. I'm sure these were hung in exactly the same way every December. There had probably been differences in opinion over decorations, as in any other household. Many other things had been slightly patched up in recent years, starting with the corners of the leather sofa. Small patches had been carefully sewed on to disguise the wear. Slightly tobacco-yellowed curtains and nets were neatly covering the bay window. All ashtrays had been emptied. The place was tidy. In fact, although the inside of the whole house, like the outside, had obviously seen better days, it was clean, tidy and lived in every day as a home should be, rather than trying to look like something out of a catalogue. I didn't blame them for one moment. This was the home of a couple who had done with years of working and were finally sitting back on life. A half-completed jumbo crossword in a thick folded holiday edition of *The Radio Times* and knitting needles, inserted skilfully through several balls of differently coloured wool, indicated that both parties had nothing outlandish planned for that night.

Objects in a room can tell you a lot of stories if you know which ones to look at. There were photographs of the couple here and there, not in prominent positions, but a couple of them were in very neat gold frames. Some of these pictures were faded and yellowing. The dullness of these images contrasted with the shinier glitter of the Christmas cards and made them blend back into the yellow and brown swirling wall-paper. I could see that every evening this room was the private domain of this couple. It was a life of their own lived exactly how *they* liked it. She had her things, and he had his. They were all set up for *their* Christmas, and, if I hadn't hated this time of year so much, I should almost have felt envious. I held a few of the photo-frames up against the light and stretched my arm to focus on the pictures. The couple certainly seemed to have had some decent holidays in their time. There were many photos on beaches and in restaurants. I wondered where the deceased had worked in his time, as he seemed to be pictured in front of some decent hotels. In one print, they were sat in a Jaguar. In others, they were pictured on the deck of yachts with a crowd of other people. I couldn't make out whether it was the same yacht in each photo. Possibly it was. Interestingly, amongst all the various images apart from the yachts, I couldn't recognise any photographs of any other people apart from themselves. Perhaps, then, there indeed *were* no other living relatives. Thankfully, however, there were obviously no children living in the house. It was not a Christmas house for children that year.

I continued my personal tour of the house, trying to build up a picture of why this rather uninteresting man could have met with such a sudden brutal end on the second holiest evening of the year, while the house was still quiet enough to concentrate in. Next, I glided my finger over the spines of rows of books in the hallway. The usual suspects were there. Recipe books leaned against cigarette-sponsored football yearbooks from years past. Complete year-sets of National Geographic magazine were next to manuals about decimalisation and slide-rules. These revealed nothing that you wouldn't find in any other house in any street. Like me, they had never got around to throwing these out and had no intention of reading them again. Next to the fat green-shield stamp-books, however, I saw a British Airways Concorde magazine.

I thumbed through this and found that there were two cardboard boarding-passes inside. Not having my glasses, I couldn't make out the printed names, but all things pointed towards this couple enjoying some top holidays with the jet-set some time ago. Down on the floor by the boot-rack were two black empty bottles of wine, each with candles squeezed into the top. Wax had melted down the sides of the bottles in the style you see in Spanish restaurants. As I lifted one of the bottles to examine the label, one of the candles came loose and fell to the floor. 'Dom Pérignon', the label read, no less. I wondered whether they had been a funfair prize at the coconut-shy. Labels like that were easy enough to fake. Either way, they were in contrast to the one-gallon demijohns of home-brew that were fermenting away nicely in the pantry. Life had certainly changed for this couple. That much was becoming obvious to me.

Their Christmas tree was positioned in the hallway, just fitting neatly inside the triangular alcove under the stairs. There were a small number of wrapped presents around it. The tree was an artificial one, a little out of date for the time, but that was perfectly understandable. Many people become attached to their Christmas trees and use them for years. Significant to me, however, was that it was exactly the same type of artificial tree that I remember having at home when I was a kid, where the stem and branches were made of thick black wire wrapped with green tape and green tinsel. The decorations had been arranged carefully and neatly, each facing the right way around. I couldn't resist touching a few of them. Instead of boring baubles, that everyone had, there were some very fine fragile humming-bird ornaments on many of the branches. These I knew were part of a set. Not like these mass-produced plastic rubbish things you get nowadays. The metallic colours were all hand-painted, including even the long beak. The nicest humming-bird sat on the top of the tree, where some people place their angel. Gently I lifted it and held it closer to my eyes. I felt it and smelled it too before carefully re-positioning it at the crown of the tree.

Looking at these decorations diverted me. They flickered as they moved gently in the air currents and especially when the two Keystone Cops kept opening the front door. For a moment, I couldn't help but cup one of the fragile figures in my hands. I just had to touch one of the ornaments but automatically felt a little spark of guilt as soon as I did. We used to admire these very same delicate little ornaments hanging on my grandparents' tree when I was a kid, and I hadn't seen them once since. These pretty little birds were so fragile, and I remember getting told off more than once for handling and subsequently breaking a couple. They were all part of a set, the same set we used to have. I remember that they were all packed in blue tissue-paper in a specially sectioned thick cardboard box. All the time I half-expected to find my grandmother stood right behind me and almost could sense her breath on the back of my neck. This quickly began to take my thoughts further and deeper back into my own childhood. For me, Christmas was a warm exciting magical time back then, and it seemed inconceivable that I had lost all my love for it. I wondered where all my grandparents' best Christmas decorations had ended up after they'd died. They must be somewhere. I wish I'd kept them now. They better not have been thrown out! Then, arriving back, as it were, I realised I was looking at someone else's tree and not my own. I looked at the presents arranged neatly under the tree in the hallway. No doubt if I'd had my glasses with me, on the glittered gift tags I'd have read something like, 'Love from Sylvia x'.

These were each carefully taped to each parcel, as if in some way a husband and wife would forget whose present was for whom. This would have been done in the same way every single year. The kitchen wall included an advent-calendar. All the doors were open. My initial suspicion of Mrs Nettles was diminishing all the time.

In the dining room, greetings cards were strung in a symmetrical curve across the pine-clad wall. The horizontal ones were folded over the large central mirror positioned over the gas-fire. They never stayed upright if you put them on anything flat, anyway. I'm glad I never bother to put my cards up, I thought. Roll on January.

I spent some time comparing that room with my own living room. But, distracted by the feel of the Christmas-tree decorations in my hand, I was soon back comparing the whole home to the house I'd lived in as a child, rather than the rooms of my own flat, which I never bothered to adorn with any decorations at that time of year. There was still something not quite right, though, about 'Nettlewoods'.

'He'd have killed me if I broke one.'

'Uh?' It wasn't my grandmother. The voice came from someone else behind me. A shivering Mrs Nettles had spoken as she was being helped along by some family friend, who ironically still had a paper party-hat on her head, the sort that you find in a cracker. She was someone else who had been caught unawares. I turned to look at Mrs Nettles. It was the first time I had seen her in the flesh. Her face was flushed and swollen, although she seemed thinner than in the photos I'd seen.

'Hello, Mrs Nettles, I'm Detective Sergeant Sonner,' was my introduction. 'I may need to ask you some questions in a moment. Then you can go with your friend here to stay in her house for a bit.' I realised that again I had not offered my condolences. I really should remember to do that. 'I hear the kettle's on.' She seemed remarkably coherent, I thought, considering the brutality that had just transpired in her house.

I mentioned this observation to WPC French and asked her what else she'd found out thus far 'between the lines', as it were, remembering for once at least to keep my voice down. WPC French was having a positive effect on me, and I began to think that she might be the one person to postpone further complaints to the station about my 'insensitivity' while I counted down the months to my pension.

'The neighbours say they hardly knew them and were not on speaking terms. They kept themselves to themselves, apart from this Maureen lady, who's with Mrs Nettles now. They didn't seem to have a big circle of friends or even many visitors at all. They generally came and went together.'

I looked over her shoulder again while she was talking. Despite the darkness, silence and cold of the night, even more people were seen hovering around the backyard, no doubt trying to get in that way. They were probably the more experienced hacks and photographers amongst the rabble. They knew what they were doing. I sent one of the constables round to the backyard and continued discussing with the WPC what we knew so far about the case.

'And close that door behind you!' I yelled at him. A few moments later I heard a shout.

'Sarge, have you seen this?!' What now?

'This had better be important,' I mumbled as loud as I could, while I shuffled with the others through the narrow kitchen instead of forming an orderly British queue. I didn't relish going outside in the cold again for nothing. The galley kitchen itself smelled warmly of roasting turkey while some rum-punch still bubbled away in a slow cooker, the lid jangling as it floated away on top. No one had thought to turn this off and cancel tomorrow's roast, given the circumstances. I saw that preparations were all there for the big day the next day. Again, the smell of the food also took me back, and I was distracted from my work yet again. I could never face Christmas dinner at my own place for this reason. I stopped momentarily once again and looked. The smell of turkey stuffing nearly made me break down there and then. Perhaps seeing the humming-bird decorations and then smelling this so soon afterwards had suddenly conjured up memories of warm long-forgotten boyhood Christmases in my grandparents' house, with me lying awake excitedly thinking of the big morning ahead. The things I see every day in my job, and I'd got a lump in my throat over someone else's dinner! Shaking myself to concentrate and trying to blank all this out, I shuffled out through the thick back door with the others. The heavy door itself had about twenty coats of gloss paint, and each coat in turn had begun to peel to reveal a selection of former paint colours to reflect the tastes of the times. The handle was of brown Bakelite with a crack on the inside. This was another repair-job neglected by our former jet-setting couple.

At first I couldn't tell what the fuss was all about. My Keystone Cop stood by the open back door, where nothing seemed out of order in the backyard. The back gate was bolted still and was doing a good job of keeping out the lurking local hacks. When he closed (or rather slammed) the door, however, there was (in what I hoped to be a lot of red *paint*) daubed the words:

YOUR TURN FOR A PRESENT, DOCKSON. MERRY XMAS X.

Obviously, with the solid back door being closed against the cold, no one had noticed this from the inside. The door itself opened against the neighbour's backyard wall, so that when it was left open the words couldn't be read. So the murderer had left a visiting card on the corpse. All we had to do was to analyse the handwriting, and we'd be on his tail. Dockson. Dockson? Where'd I heard that name?

Woken by the cold air from our various intoxications, all looked at the writing on the door in silence for a moment or two, reading the words again and again. I was the oldest and I clicked first.

'Finger-print this door. Tape off this backyard, get some lights on and sort out the footprints. Where's the photographer hiding?' I asked, knowing he was stood behind me and giving my more cold-tolerant colleagues something to keep them busy from then on. The trail was now there before us.

'And don't let those clowns get a snap of this. Clear off, you!' I growled as a press photographer was messing with his flash over the backyard wall. He was probably sat piggy-backed on a mate's shoulders. The words on that door would be in the Boxing Day papers if we weren't careful.

'Was this here before?' I demanded of Mrs Nettles. She had by then come outside into the cold with the rest of us. I'm sure I heard her murmur something like,

'I told him. We should have moved away. I told him!' Our photographer scratched his head.

'Dockson. Dockson. Why does that ring a bell?' and then he too clicked, 'Gangster!' Lack of tact there, maybe, but the others began to nod their heads. Then Mrs Nettles broke down again and was led back inside by her friend. She had shaken her head in answer to my question. I believed her this time.

We stood in the cold backyard and put our heads and the case together. The Dockson family was the name of a '50s East End protection-gang. A brutal lot they were, too, if you crossed them, and I remember they had a particular habit of using flick-razors on their enemies. They weren't around for a long time but certainly and literally made their mark around that part of the city. A few of their gang were eventually banged up, but the remainder were thought to be living from their spoils in exile in Spain. One of the brothers must have stayed living right there in London suburbia, scarily close to the scenes of his crimes. He'd changed his name and probably his appearance, but Mr Nettles now appeared to us to be one of the Dockson brothers. We'd soon get that verified. I went back inside and looked again at the body, if only to get out of the cold once again. However I wouldn't get my body warm again before bedtime that night, and I realised that I'd probably have the cough for another week. I needed a good Scotch.

Nettles, or Dockson as I should call him, was anyone's granddad or older uncle who enjoyed his TV and racing magazines like anyone else. Beneath cardigan, slippers and all, Dockson *was* a gangster and nothing less. The black blood all over the sitting room floor was the blood of countless '50s' brutalities. He was a villain. This man had been one of a team of thugs who had ruined the lives of many people and no doubt ruined many families' Christmases in his day. The Docksons had control of much of the East London protection-racket and for a time had a cut in everything that was bought and sold in the area. I thought they had all disappeared to live in Spain. He should have done, because, with a history like his, he would always have a past that would one day catch up with him. Instead, I saw a TV times, books on stamp-collecting and a Christmas tree with some very special humming-bird decorations that nearly reduced me to tears.

This was to be no less of an investigation. There was a murderer at large, and we investigated the crime in exactly the same way that we would do for any victim. But, as I thought back to the folklore about this guy, Dockson had got what he no doubt deserved. But we then had to get out in the cold and find who had done this. We had to find who had a grudge against the Docksons. There were still many fitting that bill, but we'd get the one.

Mrs Dockson, for whom at that point the punch was still bubbling in the kitchen and the turkey still roasting in the oven, would have to spend every Christmas for the remainder of her days being reminded of what they had lost.

She would begin to be reminded of Christmas from every September and would learn to hate it, just as I had done. I looked at my watch. It had turned midnight.

I want those humming-bird decorations, I told myself.

That night, as I walked back to my car in the cold wind, everything was quiet, apart from my coughing. It was difficult to believe that it was the night that it was. Adults were going to bed as quietly as their children, knowing that the next day would be a long one. I'd remembered where my family Christmas decorations were likely to be still packed, and my thoughts were towards retrieving those. Tomorrow morning could arrive as early as it liked, I was going to dig those decorations out. I decided I'd find those fragile little humming-birds, dust them and get them up. I'd hang them from the mantelpiece. They would be safe there, and I could watch them spin in the light. Instead of Scotch, my belly would feel warmer with thoughts back to those days when Christmas was the magical wonder that it should be. There would be tears, no doubt, but those decorations were going up while it was Christmas Day. I couldn't remember the last time I had cried. I needed that. The decorations, like me, needed to live again.

Terror, tinsel and turkey
Harry Riley

Alan Weywent was an overweight flamboyant fraudster, whose cut-price double-glazing company of *A-Wey-Went-Windows* went bust. He had had full order books when the firm closed down, but his suppliers had pulled the plug because of too many unpaid bills. He was faced with litigation from customers who'd forked out in advance for replacement windows and conservatories that would never get built. Also there were building-contractors owed tens of thousands of pounds for unpaid work and materials. This crooked businessman moved from town to town around the Midlands, setting up bogus companies, preying on elderly vulnerable customers and then vanishing with their hard-earned savings. His double-glazing scam had proved incredibly profitable, and he was sorry to see it go, but a very healthy portfolio of virtually untraceable offshore-accounts had softened the blow. Now he would have to lie low until the heat cooled.

Moving to the small town of Tillon on Trent in Staffordshire, he had rented a large house in a decent area and attempted to bury his past, adopting a new persona, with a splendid new name: Eugene O'Brady-Smith: a wealthy book-loving bachelor, studying creative writing. He looked for a local group of writers and quickly struck gold. Because he was smooth-tongued and used to getting his own way, it was not long before he was appointed chairman of the Tillon and District Writing Group. It was at one of their weekly group meetings that he made his announcement:

'Now please understand, I am not doing this to upset anybody, but it grieves me to say, I shan't be with you all for this year's Christmas Fuddle.' He waited for the loud guffaws and noisy chatter to die down, before pompously continuing: 'I suppose my news should really have been included in the *Any Successes* part of today's agenda, but no matter, as I've unexpectedly been thrust into the limelight: I've received a special invitation to go for an expenses-paid holiday trip to Cumbria, during the Christmas holidays.' He couldn't hide a self-satisfied smirk, as he condescendingly explained: 'I will be staying at the Byron House Spa Hotel. It's a five-star establishment, and I suppose that, as my new book has been such a success, I should expect no less. I'm sorry I will miss out on the fun and high jinks at the Old Dog and Partridge this year, but I see it as an inducement for some of you slowcoaches to step up to the mark and reach for higher things, as I have done. Onwards and upwards, eh?' And with that announcement the speaker reached into his huge leather briefcase and, conjurer-like, produced a glossy white brochure, embossed with the impressive green logo of the Byron House Spa Hotel at the top, and slapped it down dramatically on the hard surface of the wooden desk. Almost immediately afterwards came another loud slap, and then another and another from around the room, as three more members triumphantly thumped their matching white and green brochures down in front of them. Amazed gasps echoed around the normally placid roomful of local writers, poets, aspiring authors and those who repeatedly attended these meetings just to enjoy the company of others. Then the oldest group member spoke up, his watery eyes glittering with excitement and his voice extra loud, as his hearing-aid had slipped out:

'Ah, by crikey, a Tinsel and Turkey do! Can I come too!' Receiving a withering smile of annoyance from the chairman, he settled back in his seat, resuming his normal semi-comatose expression, half-rimmed spectacles falling down from his nose, to hang suspended by their chain down his dusty jacket. The officiating officer's gavel put an end to cross-table conversation, as he called for order and insisted there must have been a mistake. He suggested the other three recipients do and say nothing more, and he would telephone the hotel on their behalf, to clarify the situation right after the meeting. Eugene believed it all to be a silly mistake, made by an untrained junior at the hotel group headquarters, who'd somehow got hold of the list of his writing group's members and had over-zealously added three more guests, though how the extra names had slipped through the net he had no idea. However, the other three members who were apparently to share Eugene's holiday experience with him were themselves published writers, and they found the situation extremely amusing, as did most of the other twelve associates present.

One man, however, had been almost wetting himself with satisfaction at the new chairman's bubble being so publicly burst. He was Kevin Hargreaves, a retired teacher, and it was he who had befriended Eugene when he'd first joined the group. And it had been Kevin who'd read through Eugene's weak manuscripts and had pointed out where his plots were failing, how he was continually getting his characters' point of view mixed up and where he was *telling* the reader, when he ought to have been *showing*, as was the modern style. Kevin himself had penned a very cleverly plotted novel but had expressed no interest in getting it published, insisting to Eugene that his own writing had been purely a labour of love and written simply for his own amusement. The two pals had fallen out when Kevin, having lent Eugene his handwritten manuscript to read, had asked for it back, only to be told: 'Sorry, old lad, but I seem to have lost it. Looked everywhere;' adding: 'Of course you'll have kept another copy?' - knowing full well that Kevin would surely not have done so, his laboriously handwritten manuscript being penned on the back of some large foolscap music sheets that had been in his family for a generation or more. Then, a little while later, with a change of title and a thinly disguised plotline, Eugene's 'new' book had been published. He had received a splendid advance cheque from the publisher and had boasted to anyone who would listen that he was now a very serious novelist. Eugene had been liberally dishing out signed copies of his novel at group meetings, but Kevin had chosen instead to purchase the book from a local bookstore. Reading less than a chapter into the story, he realised with a shock that Eugene had plagiarised his own tale. By simply changing the setting, adding and adapting a few extra character names, Eugene had cleverly stolen all his former friend's work! Kevin had no way to prove Eugene's duplicity but had been seething with anger ever since, kicking himself for keeping his own story secret from the over-zealous critics in the Tillon Writing Group and vowing to have his revenge in full measure. Eugene would suffer for his deceitful cheating scheme.

Kevin's opportunity had come sooner than he had expected, when, at a chance meeting at the petrol station, an acquaintance from another community group casually mentioned that a friend of his had been booked to give a talk at their Christmas do but had suddenly pulled out on the excuse that he had been gifted a free holiday at the swish Byron House Spa Hotel in the Lake District. This had been none other than Eugene O'Brady-Smith. It had been a simple matter for Kevin's young nephew, a computer graphics wizard, to create three mock-up front covers of the BHSH and for these to be passed to three Tillon Group writers who were delighted to be in on the joke. It would be a harmless prank to play on their self-promoting chairman and a way of deflating his ego. A phone call to the hotel had confirmed O'Brady-Smith's suspicions that he had been the victim of a hoax and that it was he alone who was to receive this special Christmas treat. So, with his sensitive ego once more restored to its former glory, Eugene packed his bags and caught the early morning train to Cumbria. It was a long tiring journey, but he eventually caught his taxi to the final destination, presenting himself at reception.

Set in its own secluded grounds, accessed by a wide sweeping drive through acres of bowling-green lawns, the Byron House hotel turned out to be a fine old mansion, consisting of fifty en-suite bedrooms, many with lake views. Guests could enjoy golf, shooting, quad-biking, angling and archery classes. The spa therapy included facials, nails and pedicure for the ladies and fully fitted gymnasiums for both male and female guests. Food was a choice of English and French cuisines by Master Chef Ronalde. Eugene's luxury suite was to be on the top floor with unobstructed lake views.

The hotel reception was laid out in a comfortable country-house style and tastefully decorated with a large Scots pine Christmas tree in a corner. Lots of colourfully wrapped presents were gathered round the base. A moon-dial long-case clock stood ticking very slowly in an alcove, adding timeless distinction to this elegant establishment. Once inside his luxury suite, Eugene took a shower, poured himself an alcoholic drink from the mini-bar fridge, flung himself down on the king-size bed and gave himself up to contented sleep.

This was where he was found the next morning when the maid, getting no reply to her discreet knocking, opened the door and found him - quite dead; naked on the bed. His eyes were wide and staring, and his face bore a look of indescribable terror. Strangely, around his balding head was a circlet of tinsel and his left hand gripped a well-cooked turkey leg. A quantity of crushed glass appeared to have been poured into his open mouth.

The police, having confirmed from the autopsy that foul play had indeed caused Eugene O'Brady's sudden death and it had not been the result of a strange act of sexual deviancy, now formally announced it was a case of murder. Having nothing on file for Eugene O'Brady, they began to look into the victim's recent past and, after several interviews, arrested Kevin Hargreaves on a charge of wilful murder. Kevin's excuse that he had been in Cumbria at the same time as Eugene O'Brady only in order to visit a book fair was too much of a coincidence, and they just did not believe him. He had a strong motive. They had their prime suspect and were sure it was an open and shut case of premeditated murder.

Miriam Hargreaves, Kevin's distraught mother, was equally convinced of her son's innocence and used her influence with Detective Chief Inspector Andy Walker of Staffordshire CID to try and institute further investigation. Andy Walker had known the Hargreaves family for many years and extended his deepest sympathy for Kevin's predicament, but, having done a quick check of the evidence against him, admitted there was very little he could do. The police were being subjected to sharp budget-cuts and could not afford to waste valuable manpower and scarce resources in the hope of finding something to shed fresh light on the murder. In any case, Kevin had been uncooperative and aggressive during police interviews and had done very little to help his own cause. He had refused to name his companion, male or female, during his overnight stay in Cumbria and would not, or could not, provide the names of anyone he had met at the Christmas book fair. He admitted holding a deep personal grudge against O'Brady and was known to be a political activist. Also, Hargreaves was discovered to have a lengthy police record for damaging property and for insulting behaviour towards members of parliament in his teenage years. However, Andy had a freelance detective pal and would seek his help on Kevin's behalf. That was the best the policeman could do in the circumstances. Miriam Hargreaves acknowledged Andy's difficulty and thanked him for his offer to contact the private investigator. She would pay whatever it cost to prove her only son's innocence, even if it meant selling her home.

Osborn Lucky of the Black Cat Detective Agency had been dreading the early months of this bleak new year. Business was slack, and the utility bills still came in remorselessly. He did not have massive overheads, but, living alone, apart from his cat, in his small Midlands flat, he relied on past successes and word-of-mouth recommendations to keep his business going. During spells of intense thought, the big raw-boned Irishman had taken to speaking to the cat as if he were another human being, and Blackie had often responded in a knowing way, which had verged on paranormal behaviour. Blackie, a stray animal, had attached itself originally to Osborn uninvited and had proved invaluable in helping to solve several cases, and that was why Osborn Lucky, ironically known to his friends as Born Lucky, had named his detective agency after him, following his ignominious dismissal from the police force for ruining a big operation launched to catch a notorious drug-smuggling gang.

'That must be him now, Blackie. Your favourite admirer has just pulled up outside.' Andy Walker breezed into the room and sat himself down on the only other available armchair in the small flat.

'Get the kettle on, mate, and let's have a cuppa while I tell you about a little bit of work I've lined up for you.' The cat sidled up to the policeman, sniffed at his trouser leg and then leaped nimbly on to his knee and began meowing for attention. A few minutes later, Osborn came in from the kitchenette with two steaming mugs of tea and perched his own lanky body upright on the side of the bed-settee.

'Right-ho, Andy, you didn't give much away on the phone: what awful mess have you let me in for this time?' The police officer grinned and shook his head.

'Oh, no, you've got it all wrong, Lucky, and you don't have to do anything you wouldn't wish to. I just thought you could perhaps do with a bit of extra cash at the moment.' He took a big gulp of his brew and, putting down the mug of hot liquid, resumed stroking Blackie under the chin. The cat's deep purring signalled its contented appreciation.

'Okay, sorry, continue.' As briefly as possible, Andy outlined the story and apparent guilt of Kevin Hargreaves and his mother's concern that an injustice was being done.

'All the evidence points to Kevin being guilty as sin. He had means, motive, and the timing puts him in the right area at the right time, but his mother says there is not a malicious bone in his body. Do what you can - as a favour to me?' Osborn looked thoughtful.

'Can you get hold of the murder-file, Andy? and I really need to get hold of a copy of the novel: I have some midnight-oil to burn.' As if by magic, the policeman opened his black holdall and produced a thin brown A4 folder and a glossy paperback novel by Eugene O'Brady, entitled *The Killing of Joby*. Andy Walker admitted he had not read the novel himself but doubted it would assist Osborn with his investigation.

Two days later, Osborn Lucky was driving to the Lake District in his battered old Ford saloon car, the diesel engine chugging along the M6 motorway in the inside lane, at a steady fifty miles an hour. For this trip he had left Blackie securely locked up in the flat. He had not wanted to risk the adventurous moggy's getting into mischief, or worse, on this exploratory journey. He had asked old Mrs Baxter next-door to pop in and feed the little monster while he was away for a day or two.

He spoke to the Byron House Hotel staff and the manager, but there was very little they could add to what they had told the police. The girl who had found the body was still off work, too sick to be interviewed. It was as he was driving back to his simple boarding-house in the Eden Valley that he heard a passing car backfire and quickly vanish out of sight, in a thick cloud of exhaust smoke. In slow motion, he glanced at his side window and noticed a neat round hole in the window glass. Pulling in to the side, with his hazard lights on, he examined his body and noticed blood dripping down his pullover-front. It appeared to be coming from his neck. In shock, with panic rapidly rising, he glanced in his driving mirror and noticed a police car was pulling up behind him. A burly officer got out and strolled towards him, making signals with his hand to wind the driver's window down.

'Do you know you have an unreadable rear number-plate, sir?'

'No officer, I've been too busy to give the car its weekly - ' He passed out without completing the sentence.

Osborn Lucky awoke in his hospital bed and started screaming for a nurse. A young probationer girl came to his aid and asked what he needed.

'Blackie: he needs his grub! He'll be pining, we go everywhere together, and - and I've locked him in!' The young nurse took hold of Osborn's bony wrist and silently checked his pulse.

'Go to sleep now, you've had a lucky escape: we'll talk later.' After what seemed to Osborn several weeks but was really only two days, he had a hospital visitor: it was his pal, Andy Walker.

'You're a lazy bugger, Lucky. I give you a job, and you start backsliding right away: not a good way to increase your fee. The lady is sure to query your job-sheet!' Osborn sat up with difficulty, as his neck was heavily bandaged. Andy passed him a glass of water from the bedside table and sat down at his side. 'Remember anything about the incident, mate?' The Irishman attempted a weak grin.

'Not a lot, Andy. I was driving back to … back to … wait, I heard the car backfiring, that must have been a shot fired from a gun, as the vehicle drew abreast of me. Surely that means Kevin Hargreaves is innocent?' The policeman shook his head.

'Sorry, mate, he might have an accomplice, someone back at the hotel who assisted in the murder, for instance.' Osborn was concerned for his feline flatmate.

'How's Blackie? Is Mrs B. looking after him okay?' Andy laughed outright

'You and that stray tiger! Here's you, been within an inch of getting your head blown off, and all you can think about is your daft cat! I hope you realise that, if the bullet had not just snicked your neck and carried on out through the passenger-window, you'd have been a goner, and I'd have been left talking to a corpse!' A moment of silent reflection passed, and then the two men started talking, both at once.

'What were you saying, Andy?'

'It was just that you've rattled somebody's cage, presumably by asking too many questions. Have you any idea who it could have been?' The injured patient struggled more upright and winced as the movement caused a sharp pain to the bandaged area of his neck.

'It all happened so fast, Andy: one minute I was driving along a quiet lane with nobody in front or behind, and the next there was this van coming from nowhere. No chance to see the driver.'

'Hold on, I thought you said it was a car. Now you think it was a van.' The injured Irishman looked puzzled for a moment, as if desperately trying to re-run the episode through his mind, and then his eyes brightened and he spoke more forcefully.

'No … yes, I mean it was a commercial van, dark blue, with a round white logo, with lettering below it.' The Chief Inspector was delighted.

'That's right, Lucky: it's all coming back now, isn't it? Can you tell me more about the logo?' Try as he might, Osborn's mind refused to give up the hazy recollection.

'Sorry, it might have been some sort of animal: a bird or a chicken. All I can say with any confidence is that the van was dark blue, transit-sized, and the inside of the logo depicted some sort of white animal. It may come back later, I only caught a brief glimpse, and then the exhaust smoke blotted it all out.' Andy smiled.

'Okay, mate, that's enough for now. You have a rest, and we'll talk again. I shouldn't think they'll keep you bedridden for long, and, if I know you, you'll soon be itching to get back hunting for the varmints.' He stood up and turned as if to go, then checked himself.

'You do realise we're dealing with more than one perpetrator, unless the van was left-hand drive: our man needed a passenger to fire the weapon at you. When you're fit again, just be careful, don't go steaming in like a bull in a china shop. Just remember, Blackie needs you: old Mrs. Baxter can't keep watching over him for ever!' Osborn forced a weak grin.

'Don't worry, Andy, I'll have him with me as a minder next time!'

Two days later, armed with a plentiful supply of pills and ointment and thanking the hospital staff for their wonderful care in putting him back together again, Osborn Lucky was sitting in a train back to his Midlands home. Blackie was overjoyed to see him, jumping and leaping all over him and wandering backwards and forwards through his legs as he put down a fresh saucer of milk. It had been less than three years since the stray animal had adopted this tall Irishman: a bachelor who had never tolerated a domestic animal before and who had tried in the early days to evict the cat in no uncertain manner but who now loved this little heap of dark fur more than ever, with every breath he took. Several phone-calls brought no positive results, and Osborn began to realise what a mammoth task he had set himself. The author's murderer could have been an aggrieved double-glazing customer who'd lost everything and been pushed over the edge, or a supplier whose finances had been ruined. Osborn was still not really fit enough to get back out on the road, and it would still be a while before his car windows would be replaced at the garage, so, propping himself up on the bed with several cushions, he began to read the novel, *The Killing of Joby*, by Eugene O' Brady.

Lucky was not an avid book reader, but, during his police training as a raw recruit, eager to get on, he had taught himself speed-reading, cutting through acres of dross and digesting the relevant paragraphs. In this manner he consumed the slim novel over a twenty-four-hour period. He thought he could see why the tale had been an instant success: it contained lots of sex and violence, but, unless he could prove a connection between this fiction and a real undiscovered true crime parallel, it was of no use to his investigation. Without thinking, he started talking aloud, and the cat's ears pricked up.

'What do you think, Blackie? Will Eugene O' Brady's killer, if that's the one who took a pop at me, come back for another try? The hospital nurse did say a relative had phoned asking how I was. And I don't have any close relatives, so who could it be? The male caller had refused to give his name and had rung off.' Summoning back to mind the shooting attempt on his life, Osborn felt the blue van would throw up some answers, if only he could remember what the logo meant. Unless it was stolen, it must have belonged to a business. The more he thought about, it the more the detective was sure the lettering must have begun with a capital P, and the animal graphic represented a – a what? It was no use. He was stumped. Being stuck in the flat was no fun, and so next day Osborn decided to go out and get a breath of fresh air. It being a fine dry day, the high street was filled with crowds of busy shoppers, and a young woman was just in front of him. She was struggling with several bags, a crying baby in a pushchair and another young child holding on, as he attempted to stride by. In order to do so, he stepped off the narrow pavement and was about to step back on, in front of the young mother and her offspring, when a car driven at speed came a little too close, and the front nearside wing spun him around and knocked him to the ground. The car then carried on its way without stopping. He was winded, bruised and embarrassed more than anything, but this time he did get the car's registration details. Back home, he rang Andy Walker and asked whether he could get the name and address of the owner of a Honda four-wheel-drive. He knew he should not ask but felt Andy owed him this favour. He was reluctant to enlarge on his reasons but said it could be important.

A few hours later, Andy Walker supplied the relevant information, and Osborn was on his way in a rented car, to check out the owner. Knowing he could be on a dangerous mission, he had taken the precaution of leaving Blackie inside the flat. Arriving outside the tall locked gates to a substantial Victorian house on the outskirts of Tillon on Trent, the detective parked his car in a quiet cul-de-sac and walked around the six-foot-high walls, looking for a weak or low spot. He did not find one, but, still conscious of not straining his sore neck, he found a sturdy tree where he was able to hoist himself up and over, dropping down into a well-kept garden. Furtively crouching low, he crawled around the grounds and struck gold almost immediately. Parked outside the double garage doors were two vehicles: a Honda four-wheel drive and a blue transit van. Emblazoned across both rear doors of the van was a logo. Inside the circular logo was depicted a white creature, its large fantail in full display. Below the logo was printed the legend: Peacock's Building Supplies. Hearing a twig snap behind him, the detective straightened up and was led meekly towards the house by two hefty fellows in workmen's overalls. He was in no condition to struggle, after two near-death experiences. Jovially greeted by the property owner, James Peacock, Osborn was escorted into a lavish reception room on the ground floor and invited to sit down on one of the comfortable red leather armchairs.

'Well, Mr Lucky, it was nice of you to drop by: you've saved me an awful lot of time and effort, you know. I have twenty-four-hour CCTV around the house and grounds, and you were picked up the minute you came over the wall. You should choose your clients more carefully: that crook I did away with cost me a lot of money.' The homeowner stuck his face close to the Irishman, as his minders looked on, and lowered his voice almost to a whisper: 'Nobody cons me and gets away with it ... well, now he's got his just desserts.' Peacock chuckled and added: 'We made sure he got his Christmas turkey, though, didn't we lads? You should have seen his eyes light up! I've trailed him across three counties, and you, my friend, will have to join him.' So far Osborn had held his tongue, but now he answered back:

'I've done you no harm, but you'll be going to gaol for many years. The police are on their way. I told 'em I was coming, and they have your address.' James Peacock was still smiling.

'Okay, have it your way, but I promise nobody will ever see you again. After today you will just be an un-Lucky name in a dusty police file of unsolved disappearances.'

The following day, Andy Walker visited Osborn's flat to see how he had got on with his investigation into the murder of Eugene O' Brady. Getting no response to the doorbell, he rang Mrs Baxter, and she used her key to let him into his pal's home. Blackie was all over him in seconds, but of the lanky Irishman there was no sign. Andy was suspicious that something awful had befallen Osborn and, wasting no time in tracing his last movements, visited the local car-hire company he knew Osborn used occasionally when his old car was off the road. They were concerned about their vehicle too, as it had only been out on a one-day booking. Chief Inspector Walker put out an alert for the missing hire-car and arranged for armed back-up to meet him at the Tillon home of a certain James Peacock. On impulse he stopped off at Osborn's flat and collected Blackie. The gates of the Peacock residence were wide open, and two police cars were already awaiting his arrival. They followed him now as he swept through the drive and up to the main entrance. The policeman's urgent knock was answered almost immediately by the smiling male owner: wearing a look of total innocence.

'Yes, inspector, I did have a visit yesterday from a stranger calling himself Mr Lucky, but I couldn't help him, and he went on his way; said he had other enquires to make and was sorry to have bothered me.' Sadly, Andy returned to his car and was about to tell his colleagues to stand down when he noticed the cat had escaped through his driver's open window. The front door of the house had been closed, and Chief Inspector Walker turned his attention to the large open garage as Sergeant Wilcox came running out.

'Sir, it's the cat: it won't come out from under the big Honda. It's scratching away like mad and seems distressed.' Andy collected his torch and ran with the sergeant into the fume-filled garage interior. Crouching down, the two officers peered under the car wheels. Blackie was desperately clawing at what appeared to be a wooden door laid flat over a narrow maintenance inspection-pit. Asking Wilcox to assist him, Andy jumped up and began to push the car out of the garage. Luckily it had not been left in gear, and the handbrake was off, so the Honda slid out quite easily, exposing a solid hardwood door and the cat still in the middle of it, scratching for all it was worth. The two police officers managed to lift the heavy door away and gazed down into the deep pit, where Osborn lay bound and gagged in a semi-conscious state. It took four men to hoist his body back out and into the fresh air. With the gag removed, the Irishman soon revived and gazed at his cat with gratitude and affection: as if the animal had engineered his release all by itself! The three occupants of the house were led out in handcuffs, James Peacock scowling at Osborn as he passed.

Kevin Hargreaves and his mother met Chief Inspector Walker and Osborn Lucky for a celebratory meal a week later and praised the two men for their hard work and diligence in pursuing and catching the real murderers. Receiving the very welcome cheque for services rendered, Osborn joked that he could now afford to live like a king and would no longer have to share Blackie's fish-food.

Fatal Festival (Yule Die)
Derek Rosser

As Michael threaded his way through the crush of late shoppers, his thoughts were filled with the enormity of his intentions. When he had first stolen that kiss from Elsie at the staff party last summer, he had never, for an instant, dreamed that it would develop into a plan cold-bloodedly to murder a fellow human. The delighted screams of the children as they took in the trails of bunting and sprigs of holly festooning the lampposts interrupted his thoughts. There were still fifteen minutes of his lunch-hour remaining, and he decided to stroll through the park on his way back to the shop.

He had joined *Messrs Briggs and Co, Ladies and Gentlemen's Outfitters* about ten years previously on leaving school. His mother had impressed on him the need to obtain a position with prospects. 'If you work hard and show initiative, you could be a floorwalker in no time.' At fourteen, Michael, knowing little of the commercial world, was prepared to be steered into employment by the whims of his mother. She had herself been a shop assistant when she met his father before the war, and their liaison had led to the necessity for their union to be made permanent.

Unfortunately, that union had not been as permanent as anticipated, since his father had got in the way of a bomb on the beaches of Dunkirk before even seeing his son. For the remainder of the war, Michael had been introduced to a succession of uncles, none of whom became permanent residents. Some time late in 1942, there appeared on the scene an uncle with a similar accent to that of his favourite cowboy, Ken Maynard, in the tuppenny rush at the local Odeon, and thus it was that he was presented with a baby sister about a year later.

Uncle Steve remained a regular visitor until the middle of 1944 and was then required to join that great armada which crossed the English Channel to liberate Europe. For several months, his mother received regular letters from Uncle Steve with never an indication of where he actually was. Then the letters suddenly stopped, and his mother, in great panic, sought information from the US authorities as to the fate of the father of her youngest child. There was a singular lack of forthcoming information, and his mother assumed that he had become a casualty of the great adventure. It wasn't until 1953 that she finally discovered, through a mutual acquaintance, that he had returned to his wife in Atlanta.

As Michael crossed the park, a light sprinkling of snow was falling and, by the time he reached the gate at the other side, it had developed into a heavy fall and was turning the grass white. The children were already gathering it up in handfuls and hurling it at one another with gleeful screeches. The church clock struck two, and he quickened his pace. He had already been late back once this week and would now be due for another dressing-down by Mr Leech, the manager of 'Ladies' Fashions'. By the time he arrived at his counter, it was two minutes after two, and Mr Leech was waiting for him with a jaundiced eye.

'If you are going to make a habit of this, Mr Harper, we must review whether you are serious about a career within this establishment.' Michael did not respond. There was little point in offering excuses. Mr Leech had heard them all before and would simply emphasise his displeasure with some other caustic remark. He took down a box of ladies' handkerchiefs from the middle shelf and folded them tidily in the box.

'Yes, Mr Leech, it won't happen again.' His tormentor grunted and moved away to find another victim. He looked across the floor to 'Ladies' Night Attire' and saw that Elsie had been watching the exchange with a look of sympathy. Making sure that Mr Leech had disappeared, he risked a little wave and mouthed,

'See you later.'

His employment with Messrs Briggs had started in the 'Goods In' department, where he had been required to open cardboard boxes and ensure that they contained what was printed on the delivery-note. He was also expected to examine the contents and ensure that they were clean and undamaged. The goods inward department was dark and depressing and did little to encourage him to take up permanent employment with the firm. However, his mother had pointed out that everyone had to start at the bottom, and good jobs were not two a penny. When he turned sixteen, he was finally granted a reprieve and graduated to junior sales assistant, which position required him to carry goods between departments and make the tea for his superiors, who were permitted a short break in both the morning and the afternoon. It was during one of these breaks that he became friendly with Mr Jenkins, the senior sales in 'Sporting Goods'. Mr Jenkins was a man of some standing with the general manager, Mr Dawson, a grand personage who occupied a position in the hierarchy only just below that of the Almighty. Rumour had it that they were drinking-buddies, which accounted for Jenkins' somewhat meteoric rise to head of 'Sporting Goods'. Owing to Mr Jenkins' influence on his behalf, Michael had been promoted to a sales position in 'Ladies' Fashions', a position he had occupied ever since.

When he reached the age of eighteen, his mother acquired a new neighbour and, since they both suffered from the same addiction, they quickly became bosom-friends and spent every Wednesday evening listening to a man calling out numbers and marking them off on a little rectangular card. Their hope of winning a significant sum had, so far, not been realised. However, their continued failure had not dampened their enthusiasm for the game, and Wednesday evening still found them sitting at their customary places, hoping their luck would change.

It so happened that Mrs Morton - for such was her name - had a daughter of about the same age as Michael. She was pretty, in a china-doll sort of way, wore extremely short dresses and moved about in a cloud of cheap perfume. Michael's mother thought that they made a lovely couple and went out of her way to throw them together at every conceivable opportunity. Her name was Miriam, and, far from objecting to the matchmaking, she encouraged it and fluttered her eyes at Michael whenever they met. Michael did not find her particularly attractive, but he was, after all, a red-blooded young man and basked in the sunshine of her attentions. He never actually suggested either to her or to her parents that he would like to marry her, but somehow it was assumed that this must be the natural result of their continued association. Indeed, when it was suggested by her mother that it was time he went out to buy the ring, he realised that things were moving far too quickly and attempted to extricate himself from the ever-tightening grip. Her father then pointed out that he was not happy with Michael's toying with his daughter's affections, and his extreme displeasure would be avoided only if Michael did what he called 'the gentlemanly thing'. Perhaps Michael could still have escaped his fate had his mother backed him up in his rebellion. She, instead, took the side of the opposition, and, before he knew where he was, he found himself standing by her side in the Register Office and promising to keep himself unto her until death did them part.

They spent a week in Weston-Super-Mare on honeymoon, then took up residence in his mother's house and put their name down on the list in the hope of being allocated a council house. Some two years later, Miriam suggested that, if they had a child, they would more quickly be accommodated by the council. The passage of those two years was enough to convince Michael that not only did he not wish to father her child but he even wished that she herself had never been fathered. Following their marriage, she had made no attempt to keep her looks or to do anything at all that could be considered a wifely duty. She remained in bed until early afternoon and then took up a position on the settee with a cheap and lurid magazine, always making sure that there was a box of chocolates within easy reach.

Messrs Briggs and Co closed its doors to the public at 6 p.m., but, by the time that Michael had tidied his counter and cleared his till, it was always almost seven by the time he got home. He kept his bicycle in the loading-bay, but he had four miles to ride home. This Christmas Eve he had little time to dwell on his misery. There were so many customers still remaining when the final warning bell sounded for closing time that it was half-past six by the time he collected his bicycle. Outside the store, he could see the railings round the park and the large Christmas tree that had been erected near the boating lake at the centre. The snow was now quite deep, and his bike left tracks as he reviewed the happenings of the last few weeks. When Elsie had first joined the staff on the counter of 'Ladies' Night Attire', he had immediately felt a strong attraction. She was prettier than Miriam had ever been, with dancing eyes and a delightful smile. She had shown an interest in him right from the start and he did not tell her that he was a married man until that fateful evening of the staff party. The stolen kiss had left him feeling guilty, and he had blurted it out in a rush. She looked shocked and disappointed, and he found himself unburdening his soul and telling her all about his disaster of a life with Miriam. She listened carefully and then said,

'If that's the way you feel about her, it's time you did something about it.' He groaned.

'The only way I'll get rid of her is if she leaves me or dies.' She cocked her head on one side.

'Maybe that's what's got to happen, then.' He looked at her to see whether it was a joke - but no, there was not the glimmer of a smile: she actually meant it.

Nothing more had been said, but, for the next few weeks, he made excuses to sneak out and meet her a couple of evenings a week. Miriam raised no objection. As long as the chocolates kept on coming, she didn't really care whether he was at home or not. During these weeks, their clandestine relationship had blossomed to the point where Miriam was seen by them both as the obstacle which was keeping them apart. In a particularly passionate embrace, Elsie said what they were both thinking.

'Can't you get rid of her somehow?' From then on, every meeting included a discussion on how the 'getting rid of' was to be achieved. At first they considered the possibility of running away together, but it was Elsie that pointed out that it meant leaving their jobs and Michael had assured her that Miriam would leave no stone unturned to find him and ensure that he continued to keep her in magazines, chocolates and the other necessities of life.

Solving the problem had become an obsession, and it was Elsie that first put into words the solution that had been keeping Michael awake for days:

'She's got to meet with an accident.' Now that it was out in the open, Michael could tell her how his mind was working.

'She never goes out, so the chance of a genuine accident is non-existent. I shall have to help her on her way.' There, it was said. That had been about a week ago, and they had since concocted a plan. The plan was due to come to fruition a couple of days after the Christmas holiday. In the meantime, they ensured that their meetings were not observed and that their exchanges at work were limited to what was called for in the line of duty.

Michael did not get home this Christmas Eve until well past seven o'clock and was met with a torrent of abuse and rebuke.

'I suppose you've been drinking with that shop crowd. Don't think about me waiting here for you.' His mother was present when she said it but offered not a word in his defence. He ignored the outburst, changed out of his shop clothes and left the house slamming the door behind him. He had arranged to meet Elsie in the park and had to be careful that they were not seen. The snow had stopped, and the sound of 'Jingle bells' hung in the air. Rounding the corner bringing the park into view, he saw that the carol was coming from a hurdy-gurdy standing by the gate. This park was smaller than the one near the shop but contained plenty of little hidey-holes where he and Elsie could continue their ardent clinches. She lived in a tiny flat some three miles away but could get to the park on one bus in about fifteen minutes. He waited by the bus-stop and listened to the carol-singers making the best of their final opportunity to earn a little pocket-money this year. The bus appeared, and Elsie jumped from the platform and headed for the park-gate with Michael following at a discrete distance. Nothing was said concerning the plan until they were leaning against their favourite tree, oblivious to the cold. Then Michael went over it for the final time in detail.

'I arrived at half-past seven, and I didn't leave until half past nine. You won't forget that, will you?' She stirred in his arms.

'If I do, you will be in a bit of a fix ,won't you?' He mustered a wry smile.

'Well, we've got two days off now, and mum and Miriam's mother will be going to bingo on Wednesday evening.' She sounded a little impatient this time.

'I've got it! Stop worrying and concentrate on keeping me warm.' He obeyed.

It was after ten by the time they rushed for Elsie to catch the last bus, and Michael made his way home to be greeted by another tirade. He bit his tongue and didn't give her the opportunity to turn her bad temper into a full-blown row. As he left the room to go to bed, he was followed by another of her favourite criticisms.

'My friend's husband is earning over ten pounds a week. Why don't you make a bit more effort to get a rise, or we shall never get out of this rat-hole.' His mother had already retired, so did not hear. Michael pretended that he had not heard either and continued up the stairs. Miriam had long ago insisted that he move into the spare room with the excuse that he was a fidgety sleeper. He had raised no objection since her tumultuous snoring kept him awake anyway.

Christmas Day dawned bright and clear, and Michael set off for an early morning walk in the sunshine. Nearing the park, he saw that a small tent had been erected close to the path, and a small Christmas tree in a tub had been placed just outside. Attached to the tree was a placard, with an arrow and the legend *Santa's Grotto.* A steady queue of youngsters shuffled forward, waiting for their accompanying parent to pay sixpence for them to sit on Santa's knee and be given a small parcel containing a cheap present. He watched idly for a few minutes until a policeman appeared on the horizon, and Santa took off with his sack and the tree while his accomplice, who had been watching proceedings, hastily folded the tent and took off after him. The rest of his walk was uneventful, and he returned home to find that his mother had prepared their Christmas dinner focussing on a scraggy-looking boiling fowl surrounded by a mess of congealed vegetables. To add a touch of festive joy to the meal, she had placed a sad-looking cracker by the side of each plate. Miriam, who was occupying her usual position on the settee, pushed the chocolate box aside and surveyed the offering with a look of disdain. Then, struggling to move her bulk to a more comfortable position, she held out her hands for the expected tray. Her expression said it all.

'Where on earth did that come from?' Her mother-in-law looked flustered.

'Mrs Topham down the road had a couple of spare birds. Your dad wrung their necks, so she gave us one.' As Mrs Harper placed the tray in her hands, Miriam reinforced her remark with her standard complaint.

'If your son made an effort to earn more money, we could eat properly and move to somewhere better than this hole.' Michael felt the bile rising in his throat. What had he ever seen in her? Even at her best, she had not really been the answer to his dreams. He was certain that the only reason his mother continued to put up with her idleness and greed was that she had been instrumental in condemning him to his sentence. He felt his hands rising of their own volition in an attempt to encircle her throat and concentrated on forcing them back to his sides. She must have noticed something. Maybe she had interpreted his expression and realised that it may be politic to reduce the tension. She placed the tray on the floor. She had barely touched the food, and, picking up the latest magazine, she reached for the chocolate box. Michael rose to his feet and made for the door. He thanked his mother for her efforts and explained that he would have to go out and walk it off.

'Aren't you going to have some pudding?' He declined the offer on the grounds that he was full and continued on his way to the door. Once outside, he decided he would get his bicycle and vent his anger on the pedals. It just would not do to show any outward sign of just how much he hated his wife. As it was, he was going to be the prime suspect when she came to her planned sticky end. He kept an overcoat in the shed and muffled up against the cold. The snow still lay thickly on the ground, and the tyres made scrunching noises as he rode over the ruts created by the traffic. He had travelled about a mile when, through an open window, he heard the sound of the Queen's Speech from a nearby radio. It must be after three o'clock. He would just go on to the common and then turn round. His mother would expect him to be back for the mince-pies and Christmas cake. His route took him past the blue lamp flickering outside the police station, and he hoped it was not some sort of omen.

His mother had indeed prepared tea, and he had been correct to guess at mince-pies and Christmas cake. Miriam appeared to have withdrawn her horns to some degree. Not that she had moved from her position on the couch, but she was oddly silent. Perhaps she had been warned that her outbursts were not to be tolerated. Tea was taken in a strained silence, and then Michael left the house again. This time he walked the couple of hundred yards and entered the Dog and Duck. He could not claim that it was his local, since he rarely took a drink in a public house. This evening, however, there was some comfort to be had from the warmth of the atmosphere and the happy chatter of the regulars. He walked to the bar and ordered a pint of mild. The barmaid flashed a smile.

'Haven't seen you in here before, have we?' He returned the smile. 'Not for some time anyway.' He picked up his pint and took it to a large table at which several men were discussing the result of the local football game. He had no real interest in the subject but found himself drawn into the general conversation at the table. It was a congenial gathering, and he found himself forgetting the trials at home and the proposed means of eliminating it. He also lost sight of the passage of time and, after his second pint, realised that the clock above the bar was striking ten. Taking his leave of his new friends, he left the warmth of the bar and remounted his bicycle. It took only a few minutes to get home, but he found that both Miriam and his mother had gone to bed. He sat down and thought about Elsie. It was too late now to get cold feet. He went to bed and dreamed of the future he intended to enjoy with Elsie, following the successful removal of Miriam.

*****

Boxing Day dawned bright and clear, and when Michael climbed out of bed at 7 a.m., he found that his mother had already made a fire in the kitchen and was busy making toast. She looked up as he entered the room.

'Why don't you try to get along with Miriam? Mrs Morton has asked us to go round today and help them to finish off the chicken and stay for tea.' Michael groaned.

'The last thing I want to do today is to go round there and watch her drunken father snoring in a chair. I shall go for a ride on my bike and get something to eat somewhere. I need the exercise, and I have to go back to work tomorrow.' His mother didn't argue. She busied herself making a fresh pot of tea, as they heard the sound of Miriam coming down the stairs. Michael quickly rose and was out of the house before she put in an appearance. It was very cold, and the remains of the snow scrunched under his feet as he moved down the path to the shed. He moved his bicycle outside and rummaged around at the back for a parcel that he had prepared earlier. Tying the parcel to the carrier of his bicycle, he pushed the bike out through the back garden gate, mounted it and rode away towards the main road. Some fifteen minutes later he had reached a wooded area with no sign of buildings anywhere in sight. He had spotted the wood on a previous ride and had decided to utilise its seclusion in his plan. He pushed the bicycle fifty yards into the wood, looked carefully around and untied the parcel from the carrier. Battling his way through the heavy undergrowth, he found an ancient oak tree with a parcel-sized hole in its rotting trunk. He felt around in the hole and discovered that it would accommodate his parcel without its being seen. He carefully memorised the position of the tree and pushed the bicycle back to the road, having deposited the parcel in its hiding place.

For those of you wondering about the contents of the parcel, I will tell you now. It contained two small hessian sacks, his gardening gloves, a length of string and a yard length of piano-wire that he had obtained from the tuner on his last visit.

He stamped his feet and clapped his hands to restore the circulation before mounting the bicycle and heading deeper into the countryside. By noon he was twenty miles from home and sitting in the public bar of a roadside inn. The pub was crowded with a shove-halfpenny game in progress and a horde of spectators. He merged easily into the crowd and, buying a pint from the bar, found a seat by the fire and prepared to while away the rest of the day. The hum of conversation and the heat from the fire combined to make him fall asleep in the chair, and he woke with a start to find that the clock behind the bar was showing half-past five. He pulled himself together and put on his cycle-clips before waving at the barman and making for the door. His bicycle was where he left it, in the porch, and he switched on the lights before pedalling away. His habit over the past few days of staying out made it unlikely that his mother would be concerned about his whereabouts.

He had ridden only a couple of miles before a thin drizzle began to fall, and he was dripping wet by the time he arrived home. He spent ten minutes towelling his saturated hair and then entered the living room to find that his mother had professed herself 'beat to a frazzle' and gone to bed early. Miriam was eating a bowl of fruit-salad and custard and had her box of chocolates well within reach.

'Where on earth have you been all day? My dad says you've got no manners and won't be invited again. We've been home since four o'clock, and a fat lot you care about us being left all alone.' He opened his mouth to defend himself, but, before he could get his words out, she had started again. 'If I'd known five years ago that you had no ambition and wouldn't provide a home for me and would ignore me and leave me on my own all the time, I should never have married you.' He was goaded into retaliation.

'If you spent less time stuffing chocolate and more time helping my mother, perhaps things could have been better.' A tear appeared on her cheek, but it was a tear of anger, and she went into full tantrum-mode. He bore it for a few seconds and then said, 'I'm going to bed,' and stumped out of the room.

He was out of bed early in the morning and was washed, shaved and dressed by 7.30. He found his mother in the kitchen making toast for him. She had always ensured that he had breakfast before going to work. She gave him a reproachful look but did not mention the previous day's conflict. He ate the toast, bolted down a cup of tea and gave her a peck on the cheek.

'I might be a bit late tonight, so don't wait up.' She gave him another reproachful look but did not respond. He arrived at the shop early and managed a quick whisper to Elsie as they crossed the floor and took up position at their relative counters. 'Day after tomorrow. Don't forget. Make it 7.30 to 10 o'clock.' She nodded briefly and, on reaching her position, briefly stuck one thumb in the air. The day passed without any further communication between them, and they were careful to sit apart during the morning and afternoon break periods. They were kept busy by customers returning or exchanging unwelcome Christmas presents, and the shop was a few minutes late in closing. Michael, on getting home, ate a cooked meal with his mother watching him anxiously. Then, as had become his habit over the past few days, he left the house, collected his bicycle and rode it around the streets until he was sure that his mother would have retired.

The house was in darkness, and he did not have to endure any further abuse from Miriam. He went straight to bed and slept the sleep of the innocent until his alarm shrilled at seven o'clock. His consciousness was filled with the proposed program for the day, and he ate his toast in silence until his mother gave him the reproachful look and asked whether he had thought about what she said yesterday. He put on a plaintive expression. His mother already knew how he felt about his idle wife, and it would not do to make it even more obvious.

'If she will try, then so will I.' She clasped her hands together and smiled.

'Oooh, I'm so glad. Have a good day at the shop, and you can make your peace with her whilst her mother and I are at bingo this evening.' He nodded briefly, wiped the butter from his chin with his handkerchief and left the house.

The store was busy again as the remainder of the unwanted presents came flooding back. He was aware that Elsie was also busy. He made no attempt to talk to her or to contact her in any way, and they left the store separately just after ten past six. Michael was home by half-past six and found that his mother had prepared a *special* tea in the hope that he would enjoy it and make his peace with Miriam while it was being consumed.

'I hate to see you both so unhappy, so try your best just for me.' Michael saw that there may be some benefit in having his mother witness his attempt at reconciliation.

'I'll see whether I can put her in a good mood.' His mother beamed.

'That's all I ask for.' During the meal, he made a genuine effort to melt the icy atmosphere between them. Miriam made no real response to his overtures other than to look suspicious and ask him what he was after. He looked at his mother and shrugged his shoulders. She shook her head wistfully, and Michael picked up his bicycle-clips from the sideboard and moved towards the back door just as there was the clap of the front door knocker.

'That'll be Mary Morton: she's come to collect me for the bingo game this evening.'

'OK,' said Michael, 'I'm going for a ride: don't wait up for me if I'm late home.' He covered the short distance to the shed quickly and was on his bike and pedalling before Mary Morton was admitted. He went round the path to the road and was pleased to see his mother and his mother-in-law walking purposefully towards the community hall. He waited until they turned the corner and disappeared from view. Then he straddled his bicycle and rode off in the opposite direction.

Fifteen minutes later he had leaned his bike against a nearby sapling and was reaching into the hole in the oak tree. He retrieved his parcel and, placing it on the ground, untied the string and removed the contents. He wrapped one small sack around each of his boots, tying them around his ankles with the string. Then he coiled up the wire and thrust it into his overcoat pocket before drawing on his gardening gloves and pushing the bike back to the road. He looked around carefully, but, there being no one in sight, he mounted the machine and turned it towards home. It was quite dark, despite the residue of snow on the ground. He passed a pair of walkers but kept his head tucked into the collar of his coat, and they passed with barely a glance. Leaving the bike just inside the back garden-gate, he approached the back door, drawing out his watch as he went. The hands showed eight twenty, and he made sure that he made no sound in opening the door and stepping inside. He had checked that his key was in his pocket before leaving, but the door was never locked until they went to bed.

The radio was playing dance-music as he opened the door to the living room and Miriam looked up in surprise. She relaxed as she realised who it was and turned back to her magazine.

'Don't tell me that you're going to stay in and keep me company. Are all the pubs closed?' He made no answer and slowly made his way to the back of the sofa, drawing out the wire as he went. He coiled one end around his left glove and the other around the right until there was a two foot length between his hands. Then he stepped forward swiftly and looped it around his wife's neck, simultaneously pulling it tight. She uttered a strangled gasp but put up little resistance. Michael felt a surge of satisfaction as she went limp and pushed out her tongue. As he slowly removed the wire, he saw that it had left a deep weal, oozing blood in some places. The expression on her face was one of surprise, but there was no doubt that she was stone dead. Michael stepped back and consulted his watch: eight thirty exactly. The job had taken ten minutes only, and he was free. Despite the feeling of exultation, he realised that it was necessary to leave the scene. He took all of his paraphernalia with him and made his way back to the hollow tree where he left the wire and the sacks. The gloves he kept in his pocket: nothing unusual in that, was there? Once more he looked at his watch and realised that it would be well over an hour before his mother returned from the bingo club. He could either stay where he was, or he could ride around aimlessly. The former course was safer in case he was unlucky enough to run into someone who knew him.

By the time he felt it was time to move, the cold had seeped into his bones. He clapped his hands as his breath froze in the evening frost. Manoeuvring the bicycle through the undergrowth, he mounted it and pedalled slowly homeward. Reaching the end of his road, he was not surprised to see a black saloon car parked outside, and a caped policeman standing by the gate. He quickened his pace and leapt from the bike.

'What's happened?' The policeman gave him a look of concern.

'Who are you, sir?'

'I'm Michael Harper, I live here. Is it my mother?' Again the policeman gave him a concerned look. He turned and called to another officer posted by the front door.

'Tell the guv'nor I've got the 'usband out 'ere.' Michael could feel the sympathy in his voice as he said, 'You'd better come with me, sir.' Michael allowed himself to be steered towards the door.

'But what is it, have we been burgled?' The policeman nudged his arm.

'Just step inside, sir, the inspector will explain it all.' He was met in the hall by a younger man in plain clothes, who introduced himself as Sergeant Morris.

'Can I ask where you've been, sir, and for how long?' Michael repeated his question.

'What's happened here?' The sergeant didn't answer the question directly.

'I must prepare you for a shock, sir. You'd better come and talk to the inspector: he'll put you in the picture.' He opened the living room door and Michael could see his mother-in-law sobbing in an armchair with his mother trying to console her. She looked up as Michael entered.

'I know what you've done. She's told me how much you hate her and keep on leaving her alone.' Michael advanced further into the room and saw a blanket covering an ominous-looking pile. A man in a homburg and carrying a medical bag was speaking to what was obviously the inspector, since a couple of junior-looking companions appeared to be searching the room.

'Not less than an hour ago and not more than two.' The inspector turned his attention to Michael. 'I'm sorry to be the bearer of bad news, sir, but, as you can see, your wife appears to have been the victim of an intruder.' A screech from the armchair reminded him of the presence of Mrs Morton.

'Ask 'im where 'e's been, go on. I'll bet 'e did it.' The inspector ignored the interruption.

'My name is Detective Inspector Parker, sir, and I must ask you where you've been.' Michael maintained his look of shock. He glanced at his mother and saw that she, too, had her suspicions.

'I've - I've just been for a ride on my bike. I go most evenings for the exercise.'

'There's no sign of a break-in, sir. Did you meet anyone on your travels?' Michael pretended to think.

'Well, I did see a couple of walkers, but they wouldn't remember me.'

'Dear me,' said the inspector, 'that is unfortunate. Your mother-in-law here' - he gestured towards Mrs Morton - 'has been telling us how your wife and yourself have been having a bad time lately.' Michael glared at his mother-in-law.

'What time was the break-in?' The inspector consulted his notebook.

'Sometime between eight o'clock and nine thirty, when your mother returned home.' It was time to put the plan into execution. He put on a contrite expression.

'Well, I've been trying to keep it quiet, but I've been seeing a young lady for a few weeks, and I've been with her all the evening.' The inspector turned over a page.

'What time did you get there, and what time did you leave?' Michael gasped with relief.

'I got there just after seven thirty and didn't leave until just after ten.' The inspector wrote something down. 'And the name of this young lady?' Michael hesitated.

'Does she really have to be brought into this?'

'I'm afraid so, sir, unless we can find the walkers that you claim saw you.' It was time for his alibi.

'Her name is Elsie Blake. She works in the same store as me. She'll tell you I was with her between seven thirty and ten.' The inspector threw a glance at his sergeant.

'That's very odd, sir.' He turned back the pages of his notebook. 'A young lady of that name, who works at Briggs' department store, was hit by a bus on her way home this evening at about six fifteen. She's been in the hospital ever since. Would that be the same young lady, sir?'

Michael's mouth opened very slowly.

Meet the Authors

Annie Coyle Martin

Annie Coyle Martin grew up in an Ulster village, trained as a nurse in Dublin, emigrated to Canada, attended Laurentian University and the University of Toronto, has worked in health-care management and in the Ontario civil service. She has been making up stories all her life. Her first published fiction was a short story, 'Jody', for a collection, *She's Gonna Be*, in the late nineties. Then *The Music of What Happens*, published in 2001, *To Know the Road* in 2011 and *Between Two Dusks* in 2013.

Julius Falconer

Julius Falconer, a retired translator and lecturer, is the author of several series of crime novels (eleven set in Worcestershire, eight in Yorkshire, including, most recently the 'Sherburn Trilogy', set in 1728 at Sherburn-in-Elmete and featuring the accident-prone vicar). He is widowed, with a married daughter, lives near Leeds and is full of brilliant ideas in which no one else is the least interested. He has his own website (www.juliusfalconer.com) and is a member of the Crime Writers' Association.

Peter Good

Peter Good was born in Kenya and lived in Uganda, Kenya and Tanzania before moving to Rhodesia, where he joined the British South Africa Police Force. He served in the district sections, covering all aspects of policing and detective work from minor thefts to murders and taking the matter to local courts. His first book is set against this background. It was his children's continual asking about the highlights of his police career, combined with his wife's insistence, that made him write his first book: *NDLOVU The White Elephant*, published 2011. Peter and his wife Cheryl are happily settled now in Basingstoke, Hampshire - but consider Africa as 'home' and still miss the African 'bush night-noises'.

Peter Hodgson

Peter Hodgson is a former energy-analyst. He worked at a major industrial site in the north-west of England. His interests are many and varied. They include true crime, psychological profiling, science, philosophy and music. His published works are *Critical Murder* (2009), *Jack the Ripper - Through the Mists of Time* (2011) and *Rippercide* (2014), all published by Pneuma Springs. His interest in criminology and writing began at an early age after reading Sir Arthur Conan Doyle's *The Hound of the Baskervilles*. Peter is married and lives in Blackpool.

Neal James

Neal James began writing in 2007. Since then, he has released five novels and one anthology. He has appeared in the national and local press, and also at branches of Waterstones and libraries in the East Midlands. An accountant for over thirty years, that training has given him an insight into much of the background required in the production of his writing. He lives in Derbyshire with his wife and family. Neal's books to date include *A Ticket to Tewkesbury*, *Short Stories Volume One*, *Two Little Dicky Birds*, *Threads of Deceit*, *Full Marks* and *Day of the Phoenix*.

Andrew Malloy

Stirlingshire-based author Andrew D Malloy began writing only in 2007, when he turned fifty. Since then he has had three novels published: *Frantic!* and its sequel, *Bible John – Closure*, are works of fiction, charting the lives and times of the detectives of Glasgow's Strathclyde Police Force and their struggle against deadly assassins and serial killers. Malloy's third novel is an autobiographical account of his father's life in football during the fifties and early sixties, the stunning *Memoirs of a Hard Man: The Danny Malloy Story*. Novel number four, *A Good Day to Die*, is half-way to creation at the time of writing and should be out soon. Malloy was delighted to be asked to contribute to the anthology and describes his short story, 'The Reading', as 'revenge with a twist'!

James McCarthy

James McCarthy lives with his family in Dublin, Ireland. He has written features for the press, and *Me and the Foreign Girl* is his first novel. He was inspired to write it after reading Junger's *The Perfect Storm*. He is also the author of *The Coffin Maker*. He has a number of interests and hobbies. He cycles a lot and is also a member of the Countrywide Hillwalking Association (CHA). At weekends he can be found walking somewhere in the Dublin or Wicklow hills with the CHA. He has worked in several areas: teaching, career guidance, psychology and statistics. He has a PhD from Trinity College Dublin.

Steve Morris

Steve is a peripatetic teacher of maths, physics and chemistry. He lives in rural Wales close to the English border. In his spare time Steve writes stories. After they found their way into magazines and journals and resulted in an award, he had his first compilation, *In All Probability*, published in 2009. More darkly karma-themed short stories followed with *Jumble Tales*. Recently these were balanced out with *Out on Top*, upbeat stories of where things ultimately end the right way up despite the means. Steve's novel *Playing Havoc* takes an ironic look at a community's life after the world loses the use of all technology in one instant.

Harry Riley

Harry Riley is from Nottingham. He is happily married with a grown-up son and daughter. He was educated at John Player School and Nottingham College of Art. His interests and hobbies are reading and writing short stories, novels and poetry, touring Scotland. His published works include mystery novels: *Sins of the Father* and *The Laird of Castle Ballantine*. His short story collections include *'Captain Damnation' and other strange tales* and Pentrich revolution short stories: *Twisting In* and *Butchered & Bled for a Loaf o' Bread*. You can find out more about Harry here: www.harryspen.co.uk; http://www.spanglefish.com/lifeariley; www.millsideradio.co.uk/.webloc

Derek Rosser

Following a career as a jig and tool designer in the aircraft industry, Derek became interested in commercial computing and embarked on a second career as a systems-analyst. In 1988 he was given the option of early retirement, and this enabled him to pursue a lifelong ambition to write. He has had three books published by Pneuma Springs: *A Reluctant Recruit*, *Call Me Valentine* and *Earning a Crust*. This is his first short story.

We invite all short story writers to contribute an original short story to our next anthology of short stories.

Lightning Source UK Ltd.
Milton Keynes UK
UKOW05f0253041114

240986UK00001B/17/P